HOPE FOR LOVE

HOPE RANCH BOOK 3

ELIZABETH MADDREY

1

Royal Hewitt followed the sound of voices near the stables. He hadn't expected to stay at his grandparents' ranch in northern New Mexico, but here he was, almost six months later. There were reasons. The area was gorgeous—so much natural wonder to visit and film. Surprisingly, his subscribers ate up the tourism content. He tried not to overwhelm his feed with it—he'd built his brand around adventure activities, video games, and the single guy life—but he could do twice as much scenery as he did and no one would balk.

But family kept him here more than anything.

With the exception of his oldest sister, Azure, everyone either lived here at the ranch or within an easy drive. He didn't want to live at home with his parents—he'd moved out as soon as he hit eighteen—but he liked being close. Especially now that Cyan had married and, in addition to a wife who was an amazing cook, his brother had gained a fun almost nine-year-old son in the process. From what they hinted at, they were working on adding siblings to the mix as soon as they could.

Royal was down for spoiling some babies.

With Skye, his twin sister, engaged to the stable manager here at the ranch, there'd probably be more babies to spoil sooner than later.

He lifted a hand as he spotted Sophie Ellison in the ring with two students up on horses. She gave him her usual frown. He'd almost started to look forward to it. In fact . . . he sauntered closer and propped a foot on the lower rung of the ring. Royal fought a grin when he caught her scowl before she morphed it into a neutral expression.

"Good, Allie. Heels down, though, and roll your hips." Sophie glanced over her shoulder, her French braid swinging. "Sara, you're confusing your horse. Stop kicking his sides and pulling back on the reins at the same time. If you loosen your hold, he'll go forward like you want. Good. Better."

Royal smiled as the smaller girl got the horse moving in the correct direction. His grin expanded as Sophie scooted between two barrels and made her way over to the rail. "Can I help you?"

"You could go to dinner with me tomorrow night."

Sophie let out a disgusted breath. "Why don't you understand the word 'no'?"

"I do. I just figure it's worth asking again. In case you change your mind."

"Not going to happen." She turned and watched the girls a moment before looking back. "Why can't you get that through your fame-loving head?"

"Wanna bet?"

"Do I want to bet on whether or not I'll go out on a date with you? You know that's ridiculous, right?" She cupped her hands around her mouth. "Allie, heels down."

"Think she'll ever remember for more than five minutes at a time?"

"Five minutes would be an improvement." Sophie's cheeks colored. "Don't you dare repeat that."

Royal drew an X over his heart. "So. Our bet. Let's figure out terms."

"I'm not betting you. I have no interest in dating you—with or without air quotes around the word."

"Hey!" Royal frowned. "I'm not that guy anymore. I told you that."

"Uh-huh."

"Have you seen any indication that I am?" Royal crossed his arms. He wasn't going to go back through and take down old videos on all his social media platforms. Those were part of his witness. If people wanted to say he hadn't changed because of Jesus, he could simply point them to old episodes full of partying, bad language, and women he didn't treat the way Jesus would want him to. There was no disputing he was changed. Apparently, Sophie had done some digging.

"Not yet. But you know what they say about leopards. Take the fact that you're over here trying to get me to bet." She arched an eyebrow. "Not sure that's really the kind of thing Jesus encourages."

Royal growled. Was a little bet between friends really contrary to being a Christian? "Fine. No bet."

"Which I already said." She shot him a smug look. "Now, if you hadn't noticed, I have lessons."

"Sure. Wouldn't want to keep you from that. Mind if I stay and watch?"

"Actually, yes. I mind quite a bit. Go bother someone who cares."

"Ouch. You might want to ask your WWJD bracelet about commentary like that." Royal nodded to her wrist, smirked, and pushed away from the railing. "See ya."

Sophie muttered something, but Royal didn't catch it. He crossed over to the stable and wandered in. Almost all of the sixteen stalls were full these days. There'd been an influx of people wanting to board their horses at Hope Ranch over the summer. Morgan, the stable manager and his twin sister's fiancé, said it all pointed back to one client who had spread the word. Word of mouth was always good business.

Royal patted noses that popped out over the stall doors. He didn't love horses, but he was closer to tolerating them than he had been previously. Progress.

Morgan rounded the corner that led to the storage areas and his office and stopped. "Hey, man. What brings you out this way?"

Royal shrugged. "I was thinking of walking over to the camp to see what Skye was up to. I had an idea I wanted to float by her."

"Yeah? What's that?"

It couldn't hurt to run it by Morgan first. He might actually be the better person to talk to. He'd been around the ranch longer. "I was thinking she might have an idea of the best way to approach the grandparents about me moving into Maria's old cabin."

Morgan grinned. "For real?"

"I like it here. The videos and stuff, I can do that basically anywhere. And it occurred to me that with as much as I enjoy podcasting, I should give audiobook narration a shot. It's a growing market, and I've been told I've got a good voice." Royal shrugged. "Thing is, for that, I need a more serious studio. Something a little more permanent than I've bothered with so far. That cabin's sitting there empty now that Maria and Calvin are settled in Cyan's cottage."

"It's a great idea. The second bedroom would make a studio?"

"I think so. I haven't actually gone in to look around. I just know Maria used to live there."

Morgan glanced down at the smart watch he'd recently begun wearing, then dusted off his hands. "Come on."

"Okay." Royal fell into step beside Morgan. "Where are we going?"

"To look at the cabin." He dug in his pocket and pulled out a ring full of keys. "Then you'll know if it suits. And if it does? Just go explain to Wayne and Betsy the way you did to me. They'll be overjoyed by the idea that you're making plans to stick around."

"They know I want to stay."

Morgan shook his head. "Nah. They hope, sure, but you can tell by how they watch you, they're wondering when you're going to decide to leave."

That wasn't what he wanted at all. He'd been eyeing the cabin for the four months since Maria had fully moved out in May, but he didn't want his grandparents to think he didn't enjoy staying in the main house with them. He did. At some point, a guy needed a little more elbow room. If only so he could stay up playing video games without worrying he was disturbing their rest. "Huh. All right. Then I guess it's good I wandered into the stable instead of hoofing it all the way over to the camp to talk to Skye."

Morgan shook his head and fit a key into the lock of the cabin that sat just behind the main house. "It's what, half a mile? Maybe? Or you could have called her."

"Yeah, yeah." Royal had considered calling. "She spends so much time over there these days, I don't feel like I get to see her."

"She's committed, that's for sure."

Uh-oh. Royal looked around the living space with its high ceiling and open floor plan. The kitchen sat in the back corner. He frowned and crossed to the island. It was more than he needed—then again, maybe it would inspire him to learn how to do more than throw together mac and cheese. He glanced back at Morgan. "It bothers you."

"No." Morgan sighed and tucked his hands into his pockets. "I'd just like to see more of her, too."

"That's fair." Royal wandered to the short hallway and peeked in the bathroom. It had all the necessary equipment, and really, what more could he ask? The bedrooms were roughly the same size. Both shared the hall bathroom, which was not as nice as having something private to the bedroom, but it also wasn't like he'd have roommates. All in all, it was a great space for what he wanted. "You talk to her about it?"

"Nah. Things will slow down some now that it's September. Bookings are mostly moving into weekends—and even then there won't be many. She only put the word out about that possibility in late July."

"You two set a wedding date yet?" That was one way to make sure Morgan got to see more of Skye. Royal wasn't trying to push them to the altar, but at the same time, they'd both be happier once it was a done deal.

"We keep going back and forth. Or she does."

"About a date?"

"About the kind of wedding she wants to have." Morgan leaned against the kitchen island.

"What about what you want?" Royal tucked his hands into his pockets. Maria had left a few chairs, but he was going to have to figure out furniture without breaking the bank. Would that mean a trip to Albuquerque? The distance from a city was the only real negative about his grandparents' ranch. He pulled his thoughts away from furniture and looked at his future brother-in-law. "It's your wedding, too."

"I want to be married. I don't really care how we get there."

Royal snorted. "Did you tell Skye that?"

Morgan let out a wry chuckle. "Unfortunately. It was not my finest moment. I'll give you some advice for when you find the woman you want to marry. Don't say you don't care about the wedding."

"I probably could've figured that out on my own, man. I have sisters."

Morgan nodded. "Maybe not having sisters is my problem. Anyway, it hasn't helped us figure things out. You have any thoughts?"

Royal shrugged. "Weddings aren't really a family thing, man. That might be the issue, honestly. Mom and Dad never got married—in fact, they always used to laugh at the idea. So I get why Cyan and Maria had their little family ceremony. I can't say I really understood Azure going for the whole big wedding thing, but that might have been more Matt. Or if we're honest, Matt's aunt. Point being, you don't have family expectations to deal with from our end."

"My parents won't care. They didn't care overly much about my first wedding. They came—and that was a big, event-of-the-century type affair." Morgan shook his head. "I was still paying off my part of the debt from it after we divorced."

"Ouch." Royal winced. How awful must that be?

"Basically. So I'm disposed against the big to-do. But I also don't want to deprive your sister if it's something she's been dreaming about her whole life."

Royal shook his head. "She hasn't. My parents would have squashed that dream the minute they realized someone was having it. You need to tell her. About the debt and the first wedding. It'll help."

"You think? I don't want to pressure her one way or the other."

"Dude. There's middle ground. Even Azure and Matt's wedding, for all it was a bigger thing than Cyan did, wasn't crazy. Me, personally? I say go for something here at the ranch. Maybe spend more time planning it than Cyan did, but that'd be the best of both worlds. Say Thanksgiving?"

"That's what, twelve weeks?"

"Something like that."

"It's a good suggestion. I'll talk to Skye." Morgan pushed off the counter. "What about the cabin?"

"It'll work great. I guess I'm going to go talk to the grandparents and see what's what." Royal held out a fist and bumped it with Morgan's. "Thanks."

"Back atcha."

Royal waited as Morgan locked up, nodded, and headed toward the stable. Royal checked the time on his phone. Lunch wasn't for another hour or so. Might as well head into the main house and see if his grandparents had a minute to talk about his future.

Sophie Ellison lifted the rear hoof of the horse Allie had ridden and double-checked the girl's work. It was almost clean. Which was the best Sophie could say about anything having to do with Allie and horses. Almost. The girl tried, but never got all the way there. Sophie sighed and used her own pick to clean out the dirt and muck Allie had missed. It was probably time to have a chat with Allie's parents. They had visions of trophies, ribbons, and who knew, maybe the Olympics. They needed to understand it simply wasn't going to happen.

Not with Allie.

Sara, Allie's younger sister, was even more hopeless.

Sophie chewed her lower lip.

She couldn't let the parents keep going with the idea that there was hope for either girl—it would be taking their money under false pretenses. But how much damage was honesty going to do to Sophie's business?

"All done?"

Sophie jolted and turned, smiling as her gaze landed on

Morgan. "Yeah. Just. Still need to wipe down the tack and get it stowed properly."

"I can do that."

She shook her head. "No, but thanks. Allie and Sara took a swipe at it, but it's part of my job—part of my rental agreement —to make sure it's right."

"You know the Hewitts aren't going to be upset if you get help now and then, right?"

She did. But it was also her job. Her responsibility. Her business. She offered a tight smile and changed the subject. "Set a date yet?"

Morgan snorted out a laugh. "What's with people and that question today?"

Sophie shrugged. "Seems like a natural one. You've been engaged since July."

"Some people are engaged for years. I don't imagine they get this kind of pressure about dates."

"Maybe. Maybe not. But those people are also potentially living together. So the wedding's more of a formality and a party than anything else."

He sighed. "I guess."

"I wasn't trying to be a pain."

"No. I get that. I just finished explaining to Royal—"

Sophie snorted. "You probably had to use small words and pictures."

Morgan raised his eyebrows. "What's the deal? He's a good guy, but you never miss an opportunity to snark when his name comes up."

She shrugged again. She wasn't getting into it. Not now that Morgan was set to be the guy's brother-in-law. Sophie needed to remember that Royal was a Hewitt. If the ranks had to close— and they undoubtedly would at some point—Morgan would be on the protected inside and she'd dangling alone outside. "Never mind. What'd you explain to him?"

Morgan hesitated. "Royal's not—"

"Just stop, okay?" Sophie held up a hand. "You don't need to defend him. I don't have to like him. And really your wedding date is your business. I should see to that tack and get going. I have to put in a few hours in the office before I can call it a day."

"Sophie."

She shook her head. "Good luck with the wedding date thing."

Because Morgan looked like he was about to launch into more defense of Royal, Sophie scooped up the saddle and blankets that needed to be put away and headed toward the tack room. He could follow her, of course. It wasn't a huge stable. But hopefully he had better things to do.

The dim lighting and smell of hay and leather in the tack room soothed. Sophie breathed in deeply and held the air in her chest, counting to herself. She let it out even more slowly. Then she repeated the process. It wasn't Royal's fault that he'd shown up at the ranch the same day her world collapsed.

When her work was finished, Sophie peeked into the hallway. She'd just as soon avoid another run-in with Morgan.

Or anyone for that matter.

It was bad enough that she'd need to spend the afternoon in the office.

The coast looked clear. Sophie hurried through the stable and out into the sunlight. If she could make it to her truck, she'd be home free. At least for the time it took her to get down the hill to town, find some lunch, and get to work.

"Sophie!" Betsy Hewitt waved from the back door of the main house.

Sophie bit back a groan and slowed her steps. "Hi, Mrs. Hewitt."

"How many times do I have to ask you to call me Betsy?"

"Sorry. I'll work on it." And risk slipping up and using a first name when talking to her mom and get an ear full about respect? Nope. Her grandparents and the Hewitts went way back. Her dad had been friends with the Hewitts' son before he'd taken off the day after high school graduation. "How are you?"

"Couldn't be better. Can you join us for lunch?"

"Oh. No. I wouldn't want to intrude."

"It's not an intrusion at all." Betsy nodded toward the door. "I know you have to get down to the office, but anything Maria's put together is better than whatever fast food you settle on."

Heat washed over her cheeks. Sophie had a fondness for greasy burgers that was, apparently, well known. "I'm not really hungry. I should—" Her stomach took the opportunity to gurgle a reminder that Sophie had overslept her alarm and had coffee in lieu of breakfast.

"You were saying?" Betsy's eyes glittered with humor. "Come on. It's ready. You can eat and leave when you're finished. No lingering required."

There didn't seem to be a way out of it. Sophie bit back a sigh and headed toward the door. Goodbye greasy burger. "What are we having?"

"Maria made enchiladas."

Sophie's mouth watered. That would be better than a burger. "You're sure there's enough?"

Betsy laughed and held open the door. "She'll still be freezing at least two pans of them. It'll be fine."

The scent of melted cheese and tangy ranchero sauce hit Sophie full force as she entered the kitchen from the mudroom. "Oh, wow."

Maria looked up and grinned. "If they could find a way to bottle it, I'd wear it as perfume."

Sophie nodded. "Betsy said there was plenty . . ."

"Of course there is. Go grab a spot at the counter. The guys should be in before too long."

"Can I wash up?"

"Sure. There's a bathroom just past the living room. Down the hall."

"Thanks." Sophie wanted to tiptoe. It felt like she was invading where she shouldn't be. She'd never actually been in the Hewitts' house before. It was as welcoming as the people who lived in it. She shouldn't be surprised.

The hallway had too many doors.

Most were closed, but a few stood open. One of them had to be the bathroom, didn't it?

She stepped into the first room, hopeful. Royal Hewitt finished tugging the T-shirt off over his head and raised his eyebrows. "Help you?"

Sophie pressed her lips together to keep from drooling. She'd imagined he was fit—his clothes were tight enough for her to know he wasn't carrying a lot of excess weight. But the guy was chiseled. And now she was staring.

She swallowed. "I was looking for the bathroom."

Royal smirked and reached for the shirt that was folded on the bed. "Next door down."

"Right. Thanks." Sophie backed hastily out of the doorway and into the powder room. She closed the door behind her and sagged against it. She gave herself thirty seconds to enjoy the residual image of shirtless Royal before she ruthlessly banished it from her mind. Guys like him were a dime a dozen, and even that seemed expensive.

By the time she made her way back to the kitchen, most of the seats at the long island were full. Betsy glanced over her shoulder. "Why don't you sit here between me and Royal?"

Sophie grimaced. "Thanks. Maybe I should just go. You've got a full—"

"Nonsense. Here." Betsy patted the chair.

Royal was obviously laughing at her. He waved his hand at the empty seat, a challenge lurking in his eyes. "You don't want to miss Maria's enchiladas."

She really didn't. At this point, her stomach wouldn't be happy with a burger if she bowed out and headed toward the golden arches in town. "Yeah, okay."

Maria slid a laden plate across the counter to her. "Enjoy. Now that everyone's set, I'm going to run some over to Cyan. I'll be back in a bit, Betsy, to clean everything up here. Don't you do it."

Betsy chuckled.

"I'm serious." Maria scowled at her employer. "Leave the dishes alone."

"Fine. Tell Cyan we missed him. Let's pray." Betsy folded her hands and said a brief prayer over the food. After her amen, she cut off a corner of an enchilada and took a bite. She glanced at Sophie and nodded toward the plate. "Dig in. I know you've been busy with the horses this morning. I'm sure you worked up an appetite."

"Not like the girls did. I was just watching." Still, Sophie spun the plate a little before slicing through the chicken and tortillas and . . . were those green chiles? Even better. "Thanks for letting me rearrange the schedule."

"Have you heard why they decided to homeschool? It seems sudden."

Sophie shook her head at Betsy's question. Allie and Sara's parents had skirted the question when she'd asked. Twice. So she'd let it drop. "Dunno."

"It's nice the therapy office was able to shift your schedule, too." Betsy reached over and patted Sophie's hand. "Even though I know you don't love it there."

"Why not?"

Sophie shifted and looked at Royal. "Why not what?"

"Why don't you like the therapy thing?"

His plate was almost empty. Did he just sit there and shovel food into his mouth? Had he tasted it at all? Sophie frowned and scooped up another bite. Maybe if she ignored him, he'd leave the table like Morgan and Joaquin were doing.

Royal's elbow connected with her ribs.

"Ow."

"You didn't answer my question." He glanced at her plate. "Are you going to eat all of that?"

"Probably not. You want some of it?" Who did that? Who scoped out the food on the plate of someone they barely knew? Apparently, Royal did.

He brightened. "Really? Yeah."

Sophie scooted her plate closer to him. "Knock yourself out. Leave me one."

"Only one, honey? You don't eat enough." Betsy groaned and slipped off her stool. "Youth is wasted on the young. You ought to eat more while your metabolism can handle it."

Sophie laughed. "That's an interesting theory. I'll keep it in mind."

Betsy set her hand on Sophie's shoulder briefly. "I'm glad you joined us. Stay as long as you like, I'm going to take a plate in to Wayne. I guess he didn't manage to get through all his calls like he wanted, and I'd hate for him to miss these while they're warm."

Sophie opened her mouth to object but stopped when she felt Royal's gaze on her. Studiously ignoring him, she nodded. "Thanks again for the invite. This beats out the burger, just like you said it would."

Betsy grinned. She puttered in the kitchen to load up a plate for Wayne then headed off through the living room.

"So. Therapy. Why don't you like it?" Royal nudged her plate, now with a single enchilada on it, back her way.

Sophie sighed. "You're not going to let it go, are you?"

"Nope." He sliced into the food on his plate and took a huge bite. "Might as well spill."

"It's not that big a deal. I have a bachelor's, right? But it's not enough to work in the field. I need a master's. Minimum. And I started, but it's a lot. And I'm not sure occupational therapy is really what I want to do for the rest of my life. I want to work with horses." Sophie shrugged. "OT seemed like a good way to split the difference."

"Isn't there horse therapy?" Royal scrunched up his nose. "I really think I heard something about that."

"There is. Equine therapy is what it's called. It's what I wanted to do but it's not super popular or widely accepted and —" Sophie blew out a breath. He couldn't possibly care about all the hurdles she'd run into. Not the details. "Long story short, it's not a realistic option."

"So, back up. If your bachelor's isn't enough for you to practice, what are you doing?"

Sophie winced. "Paperwork. Filing, billing, making appointments. Basic office stuff. When my end goal was to be an OT, I considered it a good way to get to know the office and the industry. Like an internship, almost."

"Now it's just a job."

She nodded. That summed it up. She scooped in a bite that was bigger than it needed to be. Who knew Royal would be easy to talk to? Too easy. She hadn't laid it out like that to anyone. Not really even to herself. And now she was going to have to do something about it, wasn't she? "Still pays the bills."

"Sure. That's a good thing. Benefits, too, probably."

"Yeah."

"That's always good." Royal scraped the last bits of sauce off his plate. "So when will you be back up for more lessons?"

"Why?"

Royal grinned and leaned back in his chair. "Always good to know when I need to swing by the stables."

"Ugh. Do you ride?"

"Is that an invitation?"

"No." She shook her head to emphasize the point. "Absolutely not."

"Hm. But you give lessons."

She eyed him warily. "Yes."

"Good to know." He winked and stood. He nodded toward her mostly empty plate. "You finished?"

"Yeah."

He took her plate and sauntered around the island. "I enjoyed having lunch with you."

The way he said it made her sit up straighter. "This wasn't a date."

"No?"

"No. Absolutely not."

He shrugged. "Okay."

"I'm serious, Royal."

He just tapped his forehead with two fingers and swaggered out of the kitchen.

Sophie buried her face in her hands and fought the urge to scream. Impossible man. She hopped off the stool and headed toward the front of the house. The front door seemed like the safer exit.

The last thing she wanted to do was run into Royal again.

She got a brief mental flash of him standing in his room, shirtless.

Yeah, she definitely didn't need to run into him again today.

3

"You sure you want to move in here before you get furniture?" Wayne frowned and looked around the empty cabin. "We love having you in the main house. You could still set up your studio and work out here."

Royal patted his grandfather's arm. "I'm sure. I don't mind the floor—especially since you found that air mattress that Cyan was using when he first moved into his cottage. And this way, I won't feel bad if I forget to put stuff away or make my bed in the morning."

"Pfft." Wayne turned and pinned Royal with his gaze. "You know we don't care about that."

Wayne and Betsy might not, but Maria did. Or at least he figured she did, seeing as Cyan had cornered him and lit into him about it. As far as Royal was concerned, Maria didn't have to pick up or clean in his room, but she didn't seem to see it that way. And she'd said something to Cyan about it. "Still."

Wayne sighed. "I had to try. I'm glad you're staying close. And I do understand the need for your own space. I'm not sure I would've moved in with family at your age either."

"I'm what, thirty feet away? You're welcome any time."

"I might take you up on that." Wayne winked. "What are you thinking in terms of furniture?"

Royal groaned. "I don't know. I scouted around town after church yesterday. Everything's fancy. Artsy. Handmade. I don't need that. The thrift stores all run mostly to clothes—it'd take me forever to get the place furnished if I wait for the odd pieces that get in that way. I guess I can look online, but again, I'm not sure about the time."

"Which circles us back around to the idea of staying in the main house while you get things figured out here."

Royal snickered. Wayne had a point. Maybe it was the better choice. But having his own space was a huge lure. He'd never had his own. Ever. There'd always been friends or roommates or, going farther back, his family jammed onto the bus. "Or I could go to Albuquerque for the day. There has to be something there."

"That's an idea, too. Good one, actually. There are lots of options in the city. Probably could even bring things home with you."

He nodded. Royal needed to figure out something about a car. When he first came to visit, he'd rented a car. He'd turned that in fairly quickly—there were plenty of options for borrowing if he needed wheels. But he was ready to have his own there, too. So if he was heading into town, maybe he ought to buy a car and furniture at the same time. Except for the whole budget thing.

"You can borrow the truck. That'd let you transport a good bit. Or you could rent a trailer—there's a hitch. Have you pulled a trailer before?"

"It's been a long time." He'd done it. He hadn't particularly enjoyed it. He sighed. "Maybe I ought to wait, like you said. Or check out what people are offering up online."

"Might be a whole lot of driving, depending."

"Yeah. But even with gas and time it's going to be cheaper than new." Royal ran a hand through his hair. He still made decent money with his various social media presences, but sponsorships were slipping some as he moved away from things he didn't think Jesus would be on board with. He wasn't strapped for cash, but it was smart to be thrifty. "I guess I need to do some research before making a decision."

"Okay. Let me know when you want to borrow the truck." Wayne rested his hand on Royal's shoulder. "I should get back to the office. If you want company on the trip, let me know that, too. I'm always up for a drive."

That could be fun. "Will do. Thanks, Granddad."

"You might check with the guys and see if they have any furniture they're looking to offload or upgrade."

"You think they would?"

Wayne shrugged. "Dunno. That's why you ask."

Royal laughed as his grandfather left. He slipped out his phone and texted his sister to see where she was. Within minutes, she texted back that she was at the stable.

After one more look around his new space, Royal scooped up the keys and headed back out into the crisp fall afternoon.

He glanced around as he walked, taking in the scenery. The trees were just starting to turn—tinges of red or gold peeking between the green. The aspen trees would be gorgeous. He'd looked up pictures online and was trying to figure out how to work it into his video schedule. He still had about a month before things hit peak. He'd figure it out.

Horses whickered as he passed the fenced area where they grazed.

Royal watched them a moment before continuing on his way. He spotted Skye wrapped in Morgan's arms just outside the stable and made his steps heavier as he approached.

Skye eased back but kept her arms wound around Morgan's waist. "Hey."

"Hey yourself. Working hard?" He smirked at Morgan.

"Taking a break. What about you? Don't you have a podcast you should be recording?" Morgan kissed Skye's forehead and stepped back so only their hands remained linked.

"Actually, yeah. But I have some setup work I need to do—which is part of why I'm here. Before I start scouring Craigslist, I thought I'd ask if you or any of the other guys had furniture you were thinking of offloading. Wayne's idea."

"It's a good one." Skye glanced at Morgan and chewed her lip. "We hadn't talked about it much, but I did have an idea."

"What's that?" Morgan glanced at her, concern clear on his features.

"Where we're going to live after we're married?"

"My place, right?"

"That's the thing. I'm the on-site manager for the camp."

"On-site. Right." Morgan sighed. "You want me to move in over there."

Skye nodded. "It makes sense. I've been talking to Betsy and Wayne. We could take over the whole third floor of the lodge if we wanted. Very few groups ever reserve that space—and the ones who might want to could easily just add a few cabins instead."

Morgan nodded slowly. "I haven't been up there in a while, but I remember it being large. Furnished?"

Skye waggled her hand back and forth. "Sort of. Maybe you could come look? Or, I mean, your furniture is nice. We could let Royal scope out what's in the lodge, see if it meets his needs."

"Sure. Let's do that first." Morgan turned to look at Royal. "Go take a look. Anything Skye doesn't want up there is yours."

"Could we go now?"

Skye lifted her eyebrows. "Sure."

Royal waited while Skye kissed Morgan goodbye, a process that seemed to take longer than strictly necessary. Finally, he and Skye were on their way past the firepit to the trail that led to the camp.

"What are you doing for Thanksgiving?" Skye glanced over at Royal as they walked.

"Hopefully eating turkey. Why?"

"What if Morgan and I got married that weekend?" Skye twisted her hands together. "He said it was your idea."

"Works for me. Will there still be turkey?"

She laughed. "I wasn't thinking Thanksgiving Day. Maybe the Saturday after. It's a longer weekend, so it might be more convenient for people to travel?"

Meaning, most likely, their older sister Azure. Maybe Indigo. "You can't think Mom and Dad will come?"

Skye stopped and crossed her arms. Her voice defensive. "They went to Virginia for Azure's wedding."

"Uh-huh. That wasn't here. Or were you not going to get married here?"

She blew out a breath and started walking again. "They let Grandma and Grandpa come when Dad had his aneurysm. Grandma even cooked at their house. Maybe—"

"Do you have any reason to believe they've been in touch since then?" Royal jogged a few steps to catch up with Skye's angry stride. "I'm not trying to be obnoxious, but you need to be real."

Skye just shook her head.

They were quiet the rest of the way to the camp. The path brought them to the rear of the main lodge. Royal hadn't spent much time exploring out this way. Over the summer, the space was busy, and, given that most of the campers were minors, the groups were strict about what adults could be around. Made sense, when he thought about it. And there was plenty of hiking available closer to the ranch proper.

Skye unlocked the back door and pushed it open. "Come on. We can go up the back stairs."

Royal lifted his eyebrows and followed her through the kitchen to an alcove that turned out to be a narrow staircase. "This is cool."

"Right?" Skye turned and grinned. "It's very ritzy—like a throwback to the days when people had servants. At the same time, it makes life easier. We have the doors to the guest floors locked, so only staff can go up and down this way."

"Nice." Royal paused on the first landing and tried the door to confirm his sister's words. It opened. "I thought you said this was locked."

"It is. From their side." Skye came back down two steps and reached around the open door to show him that the knob on the main guest side didn't turn. "See?"

"Gotcha." Royal pushed the door closed and continued up to the third floor. "This is the top?"

"Yeah. If this past summer was an indication—and the grands assure me it was—only two groups actually used the lodge for sleeping. Most of them preferred the cabins. Maybe one or two rooms on the second floor. And the third floor—well, you'll see the layout." Skye opened the stairwell door and gestured for Royal to go through.

It wasn't the same long hallway with rooms coming off on either side like the second floor. The door opened into a large, open space. One corner had a counter with a fridge and sink built in. A shabby, plaid sofa was collapsing in the middle of the room.

"Huh."

Skye laughed. "Granddad said they used to use this as a game room. They had a pool table and foosball, and I think he said air hockey? Maybe ping pong. Anyway, it was a hangout space. They had a portable screen if groups wanted to show a movie."

"So why'd that stop?"

"Little things. People complained about the pool table—pool is bad, you know." Skye rolled her eyes. "The air hockey broke a lot and was hard to keep working. And kids would use the space for after-hours activities—sneaking up when they were supposed to be asleep. In the end, it was easier to close it off and only open it when groups needed the extra rooms that are up here."

Royal nodded. He eyed the sofa. "You know I don't want that, right?"

"Worth a shot."

"I'll help you haul it to the dump."

"Deal." She grinned. "Come see the bedrooms. Those are in better shape."

They'd have to be. The main room was bordering on tragic.

"Just a bed?" Betsy frowned across the kitchen counter at Royal. "I thought for sure some of the furniture would work for you?"

"When was the last time you were up there?" It had to have been at least five years. Royal was surprised *anyone* had been on the third floor recently. And if they had gone there? Why hadn't they complained? The bedrooms were fine—but the common space was a completely different story.

"I'm not sure. We redid all the beds in the lodge," Betsy glanced at Wayne, "when was that, hon?"

"Six years ago? It's probably time to think about replacing mattresses again. They don't last forever." Wayne sighed. "Sometimes I think the camp is more trouble than it's worth."

"Oh, now, Wayne." Betsy leaned against the counter and crossed her arms. "You say that every year. But you know it's a large part of why God gave us this ranch in the first place."

"I know, I know. Still. Upkeep is hard." Wayne gave a little shrug before swiveling in his seat to fix Royal in his sights. "Did you take a mattress, too? Or just the bed frame and a dresser?"

Royal cleared his throat. "Just the frame and dresser. Sorry. But the mattress..."

Wayne chuckled. "Looks like you're right, Bets. I'll talk to Skye, see if she wants to choose the replacements. There are some new options with all the mail-order mattress people these days."

That was what Royal had spent last night looking at. He'd narrowed it down to two. "You know what? I can find her and talk to her about it. I did a little research last night, but another opinion is always good."

"Opinions are easy enough to come by around here." Betsy smiled to soften her words. "I guess that means I'll be digging through the budget to find the money to pay for it. Did you see anything else up there that needs fixing?"

He had. But Skye had made it clear that, at least as far as she was concerned, it was her responsibility since she was the one who'd be living there. Or hers and Morgan's. "You should prob-ably talk to Skye about that."

"Chicken." Betsy glanced over as Maria stepped into the kitchen from the mudroom. "Is it time to prep lunch already?"

"Just about." Maria offered a harried smile. "The school called. I have to go meet with the principal at eleven thirty, so I thought I'd just do subs today if that's okay? I can put platters together—"

"We can handle making our own subs. Calvin okay?" Wayne cast an inquiring glance in Maria's direction.

Maria's lips thinned. "I'm not clear on the details. Apparently there was a fight. I guess I'll find out more when I go down."

Calvin didn't strike Royal as a fighter. The kid was funny and sweet rolled together. "Are you taking Cy?"

"I wasn't going to."

"Is he too busy?"

"I didn't ask him. Why?"

"I think he'd want to go along." That was a mild way to put it. His brother would be seriously displeased if he wasn't invited.

"I don't want to interrupt his day. He's working. And Calvin isn't—"

Royal held up a hand. "Please stop. Cyan loves Calvin. *I* love Calvin. He's part of the family. Don't say he's not Cyan's kid, too."

Pink tinged Maria's cheeks, and she looked away.

"It's hard sometimes, I think, to remember that you have people who love you when you've been used to doing on your own." Betsy closed the space between herself and Maria and rubbed the younger woman's shoulder. "But your brother-in-law over there has a good point. At least let Cyan know. He can decide on his own if he needs to come along."

Maria sighed and nodded. "I'll walk over. You're sure you don't mind handling lunch?"

"Hundred percent." Wayne stood and stretched. "You give Calvin a hug from me when you see him. And keep an open mind."

"I guess I'm going to talk to Skye about mattresses and maybe dig around online for the rest of what I need for my cabin. I'll be back to help with lunch. Sandwiches are my specialty." Royal tossed a quick salute and followed on Maria's heels through the mudroom and out into the slightly overcast day.

Maria stopped and looked up at the sky. "I hope it's not going to snow."

"It's September."

"And?"

Did it really snow in September? Nowhere he'd lived before had ever had snow that early. "Oh. Well. Maybe I need to add some winter clothes to my shopping list."

Maria laughed. "Not a bad idea. See you, Royal."

She launched into a jog toward the cabin where she and Cyan were making their home. He could just text Skye. Maybe stretch out on the floor of his new home and listen to some tunes. An up-and-coming band had sent him a copy of their demo in hopes that he'd feature it on his various channels. Listening to their album would be a better use of time than chasing down his sister.

"Heels *down*, Allie."

Royal paused with his hand on the door. Well, well, well. Maybe he'd go bother Sophie a little first. He could listen to the band afterward.

4

S ophie bit her tongue as Allie's heels popped up again for several of the horse's steps then eased back down to almost where they needed to be. Was it progress? It didn't feel like progress. Allie's heart simply wasn't in these lessons, but her parents didn't want to see it. Or if they saw, they didn't want to admit it. Either way, it made for frustration all around.

She tried to focus on the paycheck. Allie and her younger sister Sara were hands down her most regular lessons.

"I thought you taught on Thursday afternoons. It's Tuesday morning."

Sophie closed her eyes at Royal's teasing tone. Maybe if she ignored him, he'd go away.

"Hey, Allie. Looking good."

Allie beamed over Sophie's head and, miracle of miracles, pushed her heels down even more.

"That's good, Allie. You feel that? That's where your heels should be." Sophie gave in and turned, offering Royal a brief nod. "Thanks."

He grinned. She was sure he thought it was charming, but

Sophie knew better. That kind of thing was veneer hiding oily slick slime. "Happy to help. You want to come to lunch again today?"

"No. But thanks."

"You don't even know what we're having." Royal leaned his arms on the top rail and rested his foot on one of the lower ones. "What if it's your favorite?"

"It isn't." She shot him a tight smile and turned back to watch Allie. Sophie crossed her arms. Why wouldn't he go away?

"Hmm. How would you know that?" There was a rhythmic sound of tapping on wood—probably drumming his fingers on the fencing. "Your favorite must be something exotic."

"Okay, Allie. Switch to a trot." Sophie held up her hand before the girl could put words to the whine that had already formed on her face. "Yes, you have to."

"Sushi?"

Sophie wrinkled her nose and spun. "Gross. No. I don't understand why anyone would want to eat a raw fish."

"Come on, tell me. It's not like your favorite food is going to give me deep insight into your soul."

"It's posole, okay? And Maria's is fantastic, but it's not my grandma's. Plus, I know for a fact Maria only makes that when it's going to be below freezing for a couple days in a row. She says it warms the soul. This weather?" Sophie squinted up at the sky. "Even if we do get a little snow, it's not going to stick."

"Do you really get snow in September often enough that you talk about it casually?" Maybe he needed to rethink making his stay here permanent. Snow was fine—fun, in fact—but there needed to be some escape from it.

"Not a lot. And like I said, it doesn't stick around. It's just a reminder that you're high up in the mountains. But feel free to let it help you decide to move along."

"Wow." Royal clutched his hands to his heart and pretended to be injured. "After I invited you to eat lunch, too."

"Miss Ellison, can I stop trotting now?"

Sophie jolted and winced. Allie. How had she forgotten Allie? She scowled at the too-handsome-for-his-own-good Royal before turning and forcing cheer into her voice. "Yes. Go ahead and walk the ring. We're nearly finished."

"Yay!"

"Are they supposed to cheer when lessons are over?"

Sophie shook her head and sighed. "No. I'm going to have to talk to her parents. I'll keep teaching her as long as they want to keep paying me, but I think they need to ask Allie what she wants."

"Maybe you should ask her."

"Why?"

"Then you could suggest an alternative to her parents when you talk to them."

Sophie bit her lip. Would that be a help or a hindrance? "What if they think I'm trying to turn their daughter against horse riding?"

"Just explain that she doesn't seem happy." He shrugged. "That's the plain truth. I imagine most parents—even the ones who have specific dreams for their children—would want to know."

"I guess." Her parents never had. Their focus was on doing something stable. Getting a degree that would provide a career. Sophie fought a sigh. There was nothing wrong with that. If she ever had kids—something that looked less and less likely the older she got, but whatever—she'd want them to find a career that would pay the bills. But boy, she'd also like them to find something that made them happy. "Happiness isn't everything."

Royal's eyebrows shot up.

Oof. How had her mom's favorite phrase come out of

Sophie's own mouth? She crossed her arms even as her face heated. "Well, it isn't."

Royal lifted his hands. "I'm not arguing. Just seems like—how old is she, nine?"

"Yeah."

"Nine might be a little young to have to give up on the idea that happiness matters."

"I didn't say it didn't matter."

"Fair enough." Royal nodded to where Allie was sliding off the horse. "I'll leave you to it."

Sophie's lips bent down at the corners. She didn't want him to ask her out. She had no intention of ever going out with him. She didn't even want him to push more on lunch. It was relief, not disappointment, twisting her belly.

She blew out a breath as he walked away.

She couldn't even lie convincingly to herself.

"You're late, Sophie."

Sophie frowned and dug her phone out of her pocket. "Two minutes? That's hardly late."

Georgia, the office manager, shook her head. "It adds up. Come see me in my office, please."

Sophie opened her mouth to object, but snapped it shut when Georgia turned and bustled from the reception desk area. The receptionist gave a shrugging wince and mouthed the word "sorry" as she picked up the phone.

Today was going down in her diary as the worst day on record. Or it would, if she had a diary. Royal Hewitt on the scene during lessons with Allie. Followed by a run-in with Allie's parents and—despite knowing better—a conversation about Allie's potential that hadn't ended well and had gone on long enough that she'd had to race down the mountain to town, which, of course, had netted her a new speeding ticket that was sure to make her insurance rates dance with joy. Getting the ticket had eaten up any gain she'd made speeding in the first place and she'd still ended up late to work.

By two lousy minutes.

Sophie shuffled into Georgia's office and shut the door behind her.

"Take a seat, Sophie."

She fought a groan. Georgia had her patient-but-disappointed voice going. That was not a good sign.

"Do you want to be here?" Georgia folded her hands on top of her desk and smiled serenely.

"Here? In your office, here?" Sophie swallowed. She wasn't trying to be a smart aleck, but she apparently couldn't help herself.

"Here at NNM Therapy Services." Now Georgia over-enunciated like Sophie was hard of hearing. Or stupid.

"Of course, I do." Her heart hammered against her rib cage and her mouth went dry. It was a lie. A little one, but still not the truth. She *didn't* want to work here—but she also didn't want to be unemployed.

"Hmm. When we hired you, you were starting a master's program, correct?"

Sophie nodded.

"And you completed . . ."

Sophie let the silence hang in the air. Was Georgia going to finish the thought? No? "One and half semesters."

Georgia nodded. "One and a half. A half?"

Georgia knew all of this. Why was she dragging it out? Sophie took a deep breath and prayed her voice would be calm. Steady. "Yes. A half. In the spring, I needed to drop my course load before the term ended."

"Because?"

Because it was all too much! She'd hated her classes. She hadn't been doing well and probably would have failed anyway. Add to the top that the NNMTS bigwigs had pulled their support of the nascent equine therapy program, which meant there wasn't anywhere local for her to treat patients using her planned specialty. Sophie twisted her fingers together in her lap. "I needed a break."

"I see. And you've had one, yes?"

Sophie nodded.

"Did you enroll for the fall term?"

Sophie's stomach sank, and she shook her head slightly.

"That's a no?"

"Correct."

"I see." Georgia sighed and leaned forward. "Now, you understand why I'm asking you again: do you want to be here?"

"Yes." Had her voice risen a little at the end? Please, God, don't let Georgia think she'd been asking a question. Even though she really had been.

"Sophie, you showed a lot of promise when we hired you, but the owners are concerned that you're not committed to becoming an occupational therapist. And I have to say, I understand those concerns. You're frequently late—"

"Two minutes, Georgia. I was two minutes late."

Georgia simply arched her perfectly sculpted eyebrows and continued as if Sophie hadn't spoken. "You're unprofessionally casual in conversation with the therapists if they ask you for help."

Sophie fought back another outburst. They never asked her to help. They gave her grunt work that the receptionists were supposed to do—copy worksheets, wipe down mats—that wasn't why she was here.

Shoot. She'd missed two or three items in Georgia's list of reasons she wasn't going to have a job by the end of today.

"—and the fact is, if you're not currently working toward your master's, there's just not a place for you here." Georgia paused and held Sophie's gaze. "Are you planning to finish your degree?"

Sophie bit her lip. Here it was. A yes or no question. There could be no hedging. No changing the subject like she did when her parents asked. Her voice came out as a whisper. "No."

Georgia's nod was brisk. "That's what I thought. So what should we do about that?"

"What do you mean?"

"I mean, the job you have is meant to be an internship of sorts for someone who's in the process of finishing their education so they can work with patients. That's no longer you. You're not going to be one of our therapists, and there are other students who could benefit from the experience."

Someone was going to benefit from filing and being a general dogsbody? Who? How? Sophie certainly hadn't. Sure, she'd been in a therapy office and seen how it worked. But if she was honest, that had pushed her away from the career rather than toward it. Or was that the benefit? "So, you're firing me?"

"We'd prefer you resign."

Sophie smothered the snort that wanted to come out. Of course they would. If she resigned, they wouldn't have to pay unemployment. It wasn't as if Taos and the surrounding area was a hotbed of job opportunities. She could probably flip burgers—fast food was always hiring—but that wasn't high on her list of options. She'd done it before and knew firsthand just how hard that kind of job was. She shook her head.

"What do you mean? If we fire you, we have to disclose that when someone calls to verify your employment. You don't want to do that to yourself, do you?"

Sophie shrugged. She could spin being fired. It wasn't as if she was going to be applying for more jobs in occupational therapy. "Given the options? I guess I do."

Georgia's lips puckered like she was eating something sour. "I see. Your selfishness really knows no bounds, does it?"

"What—"

Georgia rolled right over Sophie's interruption. "Fine. If that's how you want it, yes, you're fired. I'll walk you back to the filing room so you can make sure you have all your belongings and then escort you to the door. There's no need for you to come in again."

Sophie swallowed back the nausea that rolled through her gut. Standing on her shaky legs, she nodded once and headed for the door. Had she left anything here? Maybe a water bottle? Her mind was too full and yet too blank at the same time. She couldn't quite reach out and grasp any of the thoughts that tumbled around.

The hallway wasn't long enough for her to collect her thoughts. She stood in the doorway of the filing room that also served as a break room for the therapists and looked around blindly. A water bottle with horses galloping in the surf hung upside down on the dish rack by the tiny sink. Woodenly, she crossed the room to grab it and the top. Was there anything else?

Her gaze landed on Georgia's disapproving scowl and she froze.

It didn't matter. None of it mattered. If there was anything else of hers, they could keep it. She raised the bottle and forced a smile. "This is it."

Georgia nodded and gestured for Sophie to go ahead of her.

Was she some kind of criminal? Even if she was, what would she steal? A pen? A notepad? She was better off.

She was going to be better off.

Repeating that to herself got Sophie through the office and

out the front door. She managed a wave to the receptionist, but that was all. By the time she was in her truck, tears slipped down her hot cheeks.

Sophie backed out of her parking spot and shifted into drive. She'd go . . . where?

With her foot on the brake, she lowered her head to the steering wheel and let the tears come.

flash of color zipping past caught Royal's eye. He shifted his attention away from his laptop and squinted. Was that Sophie? Why was she back and running toward the stables like something bad was chasing her?

He dropped his feet from where he'd propped them on the rail of what passed for a porch on the front of his cabin. She was really booking. Had something happened to the horses?

A tendril of concern wound through his gut. Maybe they needed some help. He wasn't making a ton of progress finding what he needed furniture-wise. Not locally, at least. Everything that was remotely interesting was a solid three, maybe four-hour drive from here. One way.

He sighed and snapped the laptop shut. He'd go see what was going on. If they didn't need him, he'd come back and continue to figure out if he was going to take two or three days driving around New Mexico and Colorado looking for deals. He could suck it up and order online, but that took out the possibility of sitting on it first. What if it was rock hard? Or itchy? There was no way to know, and he wasn't dealing with the nightmare of returns.

He set the laptop on the floor inside the cabin, pulled the door shut, and headed toward the stable with long, fast strides. As he approached, a rider on a horse trotted out of the stable before breaking into a run.

Sophie?

Royal frowned and jogged inside.

Morgan hurried in from around the corner where his office was. "Royal? I thought I heard someone ride out."

"Yeah. I think Sophie. She didn't talk to you?"

Morgan shook his head and turned to look down the row of stalls. "Technically she doesn't have to. She knows how to saddle everyone up. Looks like she's on Cinnamon. Must've wanted to go fast."

"Is that like her?" It didn't seem like it would be. But then, he only knew her from a few conversations and watching her patiently teach small kids how to ride. Was he confusing that patience with a lack of adrenaline?

"I mean, not that I know of, but it's not a problem." Morgan looked more closely at Royal. "You're worried. Why?"

Royal sighed. "Might be nothing, but she was upset this morning at her lesson. Problems with her students—you know Allie?"

Morgan laughed. "Yeah. Her parents are more into it than she is."

"Exactly. I might have talked her into saying something to them about that."

"Oof. I mean, it needs to happen, but from the few conversations I've had with those people it was never going to be an easy conversation. But even so, shouldn't she be at work?"

"That was her excuse for skipping lunch. But maybe she was just trying to get away from me." Royal bit his lip. "Should someone go after her?"

"Are you volunteering?"

Royal took an involuntary step backward. "On a horse?"

"Unless you can run faster?"

"Funny. I could borrow granddad's truck."

Morgan shook his head. "I suspect she's headed up to the meadow. She's mentioned before that she likes that ride. Truck won't make it."

Royal sighed. "Can Blaze make it?"

Morgan grinned. "Sure she can. I'll get her tack."

Before he had time to think better of the plan, Royal was on Blaze's back headed in the direction Morgan had pointed. Of course, Morgan had insisted that Royal would be able to spot the trail when he got to it. Right.

He scanned the ground in front of him for hoof prints. Not that they'd necessarily be from Sophie's horse zipping through. People rode horses around here. It was part of their business. He turned and watched the edge of the forest, looking for a break in the trees. Was that—? Yes. He steered Blaze toward the break, slowing slightly as they approached.

The trail looked well-maintained, and it headed up the side of the mountain at a fairly steep angle. Much better to be on a horse than trying to walk up it. Blaze picked her way up the trail and Royal let her go at the pace she preferred. He wasn't going to risk his neck—or hers. Especially not when he wasn't sure Sophie would even be at this clearing—meadow—whatever. It was Morgan's best guess. But for all Royal knew, she'd gone somewhere else completely.

It was a nice ride. The afternoon helped—warmish, though it was cooling as they ascended. Maybe he should've brought a jacket. Clear sky above. Juniper and piñon trees mixed in with pines and aspens. Gradually, the trees switched to primarily aspens.

It was probably gorgeous when they hit their full fall color.

He'd have to make a point of coming back. His subscribers would love it.

The trail leveled off and opened to a meadow. A chestnut horse grazed lazily on the far side of the space. Where was its rider?

Royal nudged Blaze into the clearing. "Sophie?"

She sat up, scowling. "Why are you here?"

"I was worried about you." Taking a deep breath, Royal slid off Blaze's back and loosely looped her reins over his arm. He came closer. "Are you all right?"

"Why do you care?"

"Why wouldn't I?"

Sophie shook her head and lay back down, pillowing her head on her arms. "Just go away, Royal. Tell Morgan I'm sorry I took Cinnamon without asking."

"He's not worried about it. He was surprised you aren't at work. So am I."

She sighed and closed her eyes.

Royal glanced at Blaze, who stood placidly. He released the reins and lowered himself to the ground beside Sophie. Hopefully the horse would continue to be calm and not run off. He didn't know enough about horses to say one way or the other, but Cinnamon looked content enough. He turned his attention to Sophie.

Even closed, her eyes were red and puffy. Trails from tears streaked her cheeks.

"Tell me what happened. Please?"

"Don't be nice to me, Royal. Just go away, okay?"

"Is that really what you want?"

She sighed and moved one arm so it covered her eyes. "I don't know. Probably. Yes."

"What if I want to sit here for a few minutes?"

"It's a free country."

He smiled slightly and leaned back on his elbows. He tipped his head up. The sky was the blueish green he'd come to associate with New Mexico. "You don't get skies like this anywhere else."

Sophie shifted her arm and opened one eye to peer at him. "I wouldn't know. Never been anywhere else."

"Nowhere?"

"Not really. Summer vacations we'd load up the SUV and go to California or Texas. Colorado maybe. But that barely counts. We always ended up back here."

"Is that so bad?"

"I guess not." She moved her arm back over her eyes.

"Do you have a favorite vacation? We didn't do vacations growing up. Our whole life was a vacation."

"What do you mean?"

One corner of his mouth quirked up. "Surely you've heard about our life by now? How we grew up on a school bus that'd been converted into a tiny house?"

"I don't believe everything I hear." She pushed herself up and turned to look at him. "You really grew up on a school bus? Your whole family?"

He nodded.

"Wasn't that crowded?"

"I mean, yeah, but when it's what you know, it's not too bad. And we spent a lot of time outside."

"What happened when it rained?"

Royal chuckled. "Depending on the day, we still spent a lot of time outside. It was usually better than being stuck in the bus. But sometimes, when it was too much, you just found a quiet corner to call your own and read."

"I wouldn't think a school bus would have lent itself to a big library."

"Oh, no. Definitely not. First place we usually hit up when

we got to a new town was the thrift store—there's always some kind of thrift store—and they almost always have books." It was a good memory. The business this spring with a DNA kit for one of his sponsors and finding out he had a half-sister out there had squashed a lot of the happier childhood memories. Or maybe not squashed. Overshadowed. But the thrift store trips were a good thing to hold onto.

"Where'd you go?"

"Huh?"

"Seemed like you disappeared there for a minute."

Royal shrugged. "Yeah. Just . . . stuff. Families are complicated, you know?"

"Not mine."

"Really? You're the first person in the history of time, then, who never has any family complications."

Sophie snorted. "I didn't say I never had any. But, as a rule, my family's not tricky. Mom and Dad work their nine-to-five jobs, Monday through Friday. On Saturdays, they clean the house and do yard work in the morning. In the afternoon they spend time on hobbies alone. Then they go out for dinner and some sort of culturally enriching activity. Sunday is church and quiet relaxation at home before the week starts back up. When my sister and I were born, they slotted us into the routine, and I'm not sure it was all that big of an adjustment to take us back out when we grew up."

That sounded sad. And lonely. One thing Royal had never been in his family was lonely. "Tell me about your sister. Older? Younger?"

"Younger by eighteen months, but oh so much more successful than me." Bitterness tinged Sophie's voice. "Anything I did, she did six times better. She sat up sooner. Crawled, walked, and spoke ahead of schedule. We graduated high school the same year, because she was determined not to let me get ahead of her even if it was doing something that was out of my control."

"Ah. My siblings aren't competitive like that. I think it'd be hard."

Sophie flopped back and stared at the sky. "It's not easy, that's for sure. I finally quit trying to keep up. I was never going to win. My parents were never going to see me as anything other than the slightly lesser version of my sister. And after today? Let's just say I'm grateful Thanksgiving is still two months out. Maybe that's enough time to redeem myself."

He waited. Should he ask again? Would she tell him now that she seemed to be opening up a little? Or would prying make it worse?

She blew out a heavy breath. "Who am I kidding? I'm the first Ellison in the history of Ellisons to ever be fired. And I managed it twice in one day."

Royal winced. He reached out and covered her hand. "I'm sorry."

"Yeah, well. I'll live. It's just been a lousy day."

"How 'bout I take you to dinner? I mean really, it can't get worse, can it?"

Sophie laughed and turned her head to meet his gaze. "You're kidding, right?"

"Nope. Come on. What's the worst that could happen? You're already having a terrible day."

"You know what? If it'll make you stop asking, fine. Let's go to dinner."

Royal pumped his fist. "Yes! Should've taken that bet, shouldn't you?"

She laughed, shaking her head. "Are you always like this?"

He considered, for the briefest of seconds, asking what she meant. Nah. He didn't want to know. "Pretty much."

Sophie pushed herself to her feet and dusted off her backside. "Figured."

"Where are you going?"

She turned and eyed him. "If I have a date tonight, I need to go home and take a shower. Unless we're headed somewhere that it's okay to smell like horse."

"Ah. Probably not." Where should they go? He'd have to see if any of the guys had recommendations in town. "You live in town, right?"

"Ish." She waggled her hand back and forth.

"Can I get your address?"

"Why don't you just tell me where we're going and I'll meet you there?"

"Because I'm not sure where 'there' is yet."

"Typical." Sophie chewed her lip before holding out her hand. "Gimme your phone."

Royal shifted so he could slide his phone out of his pocket, then held it out.

Frowning, Sophie strode closer and plucked it from his hand. After a minute, he heard a cackle from her back pocket.

Royal arched his eyebrows. "You have maniacal laughter as your notification sound?"

Cheeks blazing red, Sophie shrugged. "Yeah, well. I hear it."

"Tell me something. This is important. What are your feelings on clowns?"

"What kind of clowns?"

"There are kinds?"

"Sure. You've got the creepy ones that hide in the sewer, the ones they paint on velvet, the cheerful ones who make balloon animals." Sophie ticked them off on her fingers as she named them. "And a ton of others."

"You don't have generic feelings about clowns? Like all clowns are terrifying?"

She laughed. "No. But now I know what to get you for your birthday."

Royal shuddered and checked his texts. "You still didn't put your address in."

"True. But now you can text me where we're meeting."

"Are you always like this?"

"Yeah, pretty much." She grinned and pointed at him. "But you cheered me up, and I didn't think that was possible today, so I'll try to tone it down at dinner."

He'd cheered her up. And they'd actually had a decent conversation, which was a first. Unfortunately, it didn't help convince Royal that he should let her be.

If anything, the more he learned about Sophie Ellison, the more he wanted to know.

6

W hat had she been thinking?

Sophie frowned at the clothes in her closet. She didn't have date clothes. She had horse riding clothes. And business casual office clothes. And the flowery skirt her mom had bought her for Easter last year.

Wrinkling her nose, Sophie reached for the skirt. Was it as awful as she remembered? She squinted at it. Maybe it wasn't awful? There was a lightweight mock turtleneck sweater that went with it. The whole thing felt very . . . girly. It was something her sister would adore.

Was that the problem she had with it?

She blew out a breath and considered the row of shoes lined up on the floor. The suede knee boots she'd bought for family photos last year would work. And they'd make the outfit a little more her. Mom would expect her to wear pumps—some kind of mile-high heel with an open toe. Too bad she was fresh out.

Sophie changed and stared at herself in the bathroom mirror. She poked at her belly. She really needed to start doing sit-ups again. Or something. Maybe now that she had all this free time, she could focus on getting a little more fit. Not that she'd be unemployed forever. Tomorrow she would have to start looking for a job.

She closed her eyes and pushed at the dread that filled her. She was going to end up flipping burgers or waiting tables. Without a master's, she officially had a useless college degree.

Her phone cackled and her lips twitched involuntarily as she thought about Royal's reaction to the sound. Maybe maniacal clowns were strange, but, to her at least, it was a cheerful sound. And she never had to worry about mistaking her phone for someone else's.

You sure I can't pick you up?

Sophie frowned. Yes, she was sure. Was persistence a good thing? Or an annoying one? Maybe it could be both. She tapped out her reply.

Yes. Just tell me where we're going and what time to be there.

After almost a minute, another text came through with an address. Sophie drew her eyebrows together. It wasn't familiar. She tapped to open it in her mapping app and blinked. No way was he taking her there.

She hit the call button, her frown deepening as it rang.

"Hey. I was just sending the reservation time."

"Royal. There's no way. That place is super fancy." And expensive. She wasn't going to say that part. Presumably he checked it out ahead of time. But if not, mentioning fancy ought to be a clue.

"I have a tie on and everything. The menu made my mouth water."

The food was supposed to be amazing. She hadn't actually been there before. Dad took Mom there once a year for their anniversary. And they'd taken her sister when she graduated from college. They hadn't taken Sophie, because she still had to finish her master's before she was employable. That was, if not a direct quote, close enough. "I just—it's not a first date kind of place."

"So this is our first date?" Sophie could hear the grin in his voice.

She covered her face with her hands. "Is there any way for me to win this argument?"

"Do you really want to?"

Did she? Everything she'd looked up about Royal—and it had been more than she'd ever admit out loud—said he was just the kind of guy she should run away from. Possibly while screaming. But none of that jibed with the person she'd seen at the ranch. He'd been around since the spring. And he seemed normal. Fun. And solid.

None of his recent videos or podcasts showed the guy he'd been before, either.

So did she want to win the argument?

"No. I guess I don't."

"Cool. So, you'll text me your address?"

Give the man an inch. She sighed. "Fine. I'm about ten minutes in the other direction from the restaurant. So you'll need to leave soon."

"I'll see you in about twenty."

"Sounds good." Sophie ended the call and sank onto the foot of her bed. She buried her face in her hands and groaned. What was she doing? Dating Royal Hewitt was a recipe for heartbreak.

"WHAT WILL YOU DO?" Royal reached into the basket of *sopapillas* that they'd agreed to share for dessert.

Sophie waited to see what he was going to do. He tore off a corner and drizzled honey inside like a native. She grinned. "You've done this before."

"Maria makes them. She gave me a tutorial. They're a favorite now." He pointed the doughy treat at her. "You didn't answer the question."

"That's because I don't know." Sophie grabbed her own treat and bit off one of the pointed ends. "Find a job is number one on the to-do list. I'll figure something out tomorrow. I still have a couple of riding lessons, so I'll need to be able to work around them, but I can probably shift everyone to Saturdays."

Royal nodded. "You won't try to find new students?"

"I'm always looking for new students. It's just hard to drum them up. We're a small community. A lot of the people who have horses have their own stable. Their own land. And a parent or someone in the family who knows horses and does the instruction. Then you've got the people who want to learn to ride who are friends with the first group of people." She shrugged. "By the time you get to someone who wants to pay for lessons, there are a lot of options for them to choose from. It's hard for me to compete. I don't have my own space and horses. I'm seriously blessed that the Hewitts made their arrangement with me as reasonable as they did. And the reality is, I still need to work. I've got bills that have to get paid."

"Makes sense."

Sophie shifted so she could look out across the patio to the mountains rising in the distance. "If I was smart, I'd move. Head to Albuquerque. Or at least Santa Fe. Somewhere with more opportunities. But I don't want to leave."

"You'll notice I stuck around." Royal smiled and reached across the table. He covered her hand with his own.

Sophie stilled and glanced down at their hands. His skin was warm. Now her skin was warm. And tingly. She cleared her throat. "Because of the area?"

"That was a factor, for sure." He sighed and curved his fingers more tightly around her hand. "Now I'm working on getting a cabin set up—my grandparents said I could live in Maria's old place, since she and Calvin are living in Cyan's cottage."

"How's that going?" Of course he was staying. Because she couldn't catch a break.

He waggled his free hand side to side. "Furniture isn't a super big deal. I got a bed frame from the camp. Ordered a mattress online—it's pretty comfy. I need some basic living room stuff. I'm looking at yard sale websites. But what I really want to do is outfit the second bedroom as a recording studio."

Her eyebrows lifted. "That's ambitious."

"Not really. I could probably order good enough online for under a grand. And make it work. But there's this guy in Arizona —just over the border according to the map I looked at—and he's selling a whole kit. Professional grade. For about what I'd spend for the hobby-level stuff."

"Nice. What's the problem?"

"It'd be a couple day trip—a day out, a day back for sure. But if I'm going all that way, I should take the extra time to go see my sister and parents. And I'd need to pull a trailer. Plus borrow one of the ranch trucks for that long. Or rent something. I don't know. It seems like a lot."

"But it's better equipment?"

"Oh yeah. A ton better."

"I'll take you." Sophie pressed her lips together. What? What did she just say? Obviously the cool breeze and candlelight had gone to her head. Or she'd completely lost her mind. She did not want to spend a couple of days with Royal on a road trip. *Please say no. Please say no.*

"You will? Really? That'd be amazing." He grinned at her.

Sophie's breath caught. His smile was lethal when he turned on the charm. It had to be conscious. And yet, she melted. "When would you want to leave?"

SOPHIE TAPPED a few keys on her laptop and reached for her coffee. That was the most positive spin she could put on her work experience. As she sipped, she read over the listing of all her jobs and sighed. She wouldn't hire her, so why would anyone else?

What did she even want to do? Work with horses. Teach people—preferably kids—how to ride them. Hippotherapy.

Chances of making any of those dreams come true? Slim to none.

She could reach out to some of the stables in the area. Maybe they were looking for another instructor, but it was unlikely.

Sophie pushed away from the table, hit Save, and stood. She carried her coffee to the sliding glass door that looked out over what her apartment complex laughingly called a patio. After unlocking it, she slid the door open and stepped out. Crisp air that bordered on cold filled her lungs. Goosebumps puckered on her arms. Tiny hints of fall color were visible on the mountainside in the distance. It wouldn't be long before red and orange were the dominant hues. Then the leaves would fall and the snow would start.

Would she still be here, in this apartment, then? Not if she couldn't find a job.

There was a knock at her door.

Sophie stepped back inside, took a second to lock the door, and crossed the main room of her apartment to peek at who was visiting her on a Wednesday morning.

Pasting on a smile, she pulled open the door. "Hi, Mom."

"Hello, honey." Her mother swept in, pressing a kiss to Sophie's cheek as she passed. She stopped and surveyed her daughter's apartment with a slight shake of her head. "I still don't understand why you don't live at home until you can afford a real house."

Sophie shut the door and drained her coffee. She wasn't going to engage in that conversation again. "Can I get you something to drink? There's coffee. Or I can make some tea?"

"No, thank you. I can't stay. I'm on my way to church for the women's Bible study." Her mom turned and tilted her head to the side. "I didn't actually think I'd find you at home."

"Sure you did." Sophie gestured to the secondhand couch that she'd covered with blankets from a thrift store. "I'm sure Allie's parents called you. They've been family friends for years."

"Well, their parents have, yes." Her mom perched on the edge of the sofa and sighed. "You couldn't just keep giving the girls lessons?"

"I'm not the one who ended lessons."

Her mother waved that away. "Maybe you didn't outright say you wanted to stop teaching, but when you tell them there's no chance the girls are going to be any good, what did you expect?"

"I didn't say that, either. What I said was that I didn't see the Olympics—or any other competition—in either girl's future. Neither Allie nor Sara wants it enough. And only Sara has even the tiniest bit of talent. If they were enjoying the lessons—if riding or even being around horses was an interest the girls had —I'd be more than happy to keep teaching them. But Mom, it's dishonest to keep teaching them without letting their parents know reality."

"I suppose. It's going to make things awkward for your father and me."

Sophie glanced into her empty mug. Why hadn't she refilled it before sitting down? "How?"

"You fired our friends' grandchildren!"

"I just explained—never mind. I take it that's the narrative that's going around?" If that was the case, she could cross off contacting the local stables. No one was going to hire her as an instructor if she had a reputation for firing students. She shook her head. "Typical."

"What's typical, Sophie? That you got yourself in trouble because you spoke before you thought?"

Shock had Sophie's jaw dropping. Her eyes burned as they filled. "That's not what happened!"

"It's what they're saying happened, so it's basically the same thing."

"Why can't you ever take my side? Or even withhold judgment until you know my side? Why is that, Mom?" Sophie stood and paced to the coffee maker. She set her mug on the counter and swallowed. Her stomach twisted. "I guess you might as well know I also lost my job at the physical therapy office yesterday."

"Oh, Sophie." Her mother twisted around so their eyes met. "When are you going to learn?"

"To learn what, Mom? You think I got let go because of something I said?"

"Didn't you?"

In reality, it could be interpreted that way. Sophie had said she didn't want to finish her master's degree. "No. I didn't. But it's not like I expect you to believe me."

"It had to be something. People don't just go around firing employees."

"They do when the employee is no longer pursuing the degree that's needed in the field."

Her mother's shoulders dropped, and she pushed to her feet. "I thought you were going to enroll for the fall term."

Sophie just shook her head. There was no explanation, no justification that was going to appease her mom. It was why she hadn't said anything. "Dad knows."

Her mom frowned.

"When we talked about it, he agreed that it was the right choice."

"So what will you do?" Her mother shook her head. "You'll move back home, of course. We'll come this weekend to help you pack."

"No, Mom. I won't. I'll find something else. I have enough to keep paying rent for a while. It's going to be okay." At least, that was what she kept telling herself. Maybe if she could convince her mom, Sophie would be able to believe it herself.

"You know I love you, Sophie."

Despite everything, she did. Sophie nodded.

"We'd love to have you back home. It's really no problem."

"I'll keep that in mind, but I'm going to be fine." Sophie's smile was a little more genuine this time.

"All right. Will you tell me if you're not. Or at least tell Dad?"

"You'll be the first." Well, maybe not the first. But she'd get to them. Eventually.

"I just don't understand why you can't be more like your sister."

"I know. Have fun at Bible study."

Her mom kissed Sophie's cheek. "Come to dinner some night soon."

"I'll let you know."

Her mother nodded and left.

Sophie blew out a breath. There had to be a bright side, didn't there? She ran a hand through her hair and laughed. Maybe the bright side was that Mom found out before Sophie had to be the one to tell them.

Or maybe it was that somehow her mother hadn't found out about her date with Royal.

At least not yet.

7

"You need to go see her, Royal." Skye scowled at him, her hands on her hips. "You're the first person who's going to be remotely close enough. She's making the effort to come this far, we can meet her halfway."

"I don't want to meet her." Royal tossed another pair of jeans into the duffel bag he was packing. "Look, Sophie agreed to drive me out to get the recording equipment. I could tell she regretted it almost the minute the words were out of her mouth. I'm not pushing her to make yet another side trip when we're already going the long way so we can stop and see Mom and Dad and maybe Indigo before we pick up the equipment."

"But that's just it! Leaving from Mom and Dad's, you'll have to go through Phoenix to get to the equipment anyway. And Jade's driving out from Los Angeles. It really is the least you can do."

Royal frowned at his twin. "There are other, faster routes to the equipment."

"Faster by what, five minutes?"

Closer to thirty. But his sister wasn't likely to feel that was enough to make a difference. And she probably had a point. He sank onto the bed beside his duffel. "I still don't see why this is my responsibility. If she's going to Phoenix, that means she's heading up to see Mom and Dad, right?"

"I'm hoping we can head that off at the pass."

"Ah." Now it made more sense. "Why not just let her go up there? Isn't that what she wants?"

"You really think that's a good idea? After Dad had an aneurysm in the spring? He can still barely get around. And Mom isn't doing well."

"What's wrong with Mom?"

"This whole thing with Jade. She refuses to talk about it—just pretends like nothing happened and Jade doesn't exist. Dad is following Mom's lead. What's going to happen if Jade shows up on their doorstep and forces the issue?" Skye threw her hands in the air. "Do you *want* Dad to have a stroke?"

"To be fair, Mom might just kill him."

"It's not a joke, Royal."

He held up his hands. "Okay. Okay. Bad timing. I still don't see why I have to do this."

"Because you're already going to be out there. I could make the time to go if Jade had waited until November, but we've got retreats at the lodge booked through mid-October."

That was a good thing. And it was all Skye's doing. She'd been the one to suggest to their grandparents that they could do more with the camp—particularly the lodge—in what had been their off-season. Skye had spent a lot of time talking to their oldest sister, Azure, and the rest of the Peacock Hill gang over the summer. The trip to Azure's wedding over Labor Day had cemented it. "So Cyan should go."

Skye snorted. "Cyan. You've met our brother, right? Do you really think he has the diplomatic skills to be the first of us to meet our half-sister in person?"

"Yeah, okay. That's a point." Royal ran a hand through his hair. "Why me?"

"You're a better choice than Indigo. She's got enough trouble anyway."

"Still nothing from Wingfeather?"

Skye shook her head. "Not a peep. He's been out of touch since early July. She's starting to get worried."

"Almost three months and now she's getting worried?" Royal was never going to understand Indigo.

Skye shrugged. "I guess that's their relationship. Maybe it wasn't always that way, but I'm glad you're going to see her. She could use a hug. But you also see why I need to keep Jade out of all this. Right?"

"I guess. Why is she even coming to Arizona?"

"She has a work thing in Phoenix. I must have let slip at some point that Mom and Dad were nearby. She's been pushing for their contact info ever since. If I can tell her you'll meet her —take her to dinner—maybe that'll put off the inevitable."

"For how long? It's not going to be hard for her to figure out where Mom and Dad are."

Skye sighed. "I know. I just—now isn't the time. Mom and Dad need to figure out where they stand on the whole thing before she just shows up."

"I take it you expect me to fix that while I'm there, too?"

Skye beamed at him. "Would you?"

Royal snorted. He'd walked right into that one. "I'll see what I can do. No promises."

"Thanks, Royal." Skye laid her hand on his arm. "Seriously."

"You owe me."

"Nah." She grinned. "Sister privileges."

Royal zipped the bag and glared at Skye. "Are you ever going to grow out of that?"

"No. Why would I?" She wrapped her arms around Royal

and squeezed before digging her fingers into his side at his most ticklish spot. "It always works."

"Stop!" Royal wriggled out of her grasp and slapped at her hands, laughing. "Skye, I'm serious. Stop. Grow up."

Laughing, Skye held up her hands. "All right. I stopped. Thanks. Seriously."

"Yeah, well, you might want to save the thanks until you know if I do any good." Royal scanned the room for anything else he might need to take on this trip. He'd spent the four days since their date looking forward to time alone with Sophie— especially once it started to seem like she was avoiding him. Now, nerves churned in his stomach.

Airing the family dirty laundry in front of the girl he was crushing on was way, way low on the list of things he was excited to do.

ROYAL CARRIED the bag of hamburgers and fries in one hand and balanced the drink carrier in the other as he crossed the parking lot. Sophie had parked her truck and was waiting. He could see her drumming her fingers on the steering wheel. The drive-through line wrapped almost around the building, but inside at the counter had moved quickly.

Sophie leaned over and pushed open the passenger door. "That was fast."

"Told you." He held out the drink carrier and waited until she'd grasped it to climb in. "People leaving church want the drive-through. They don't want to eat in unless they're going to a sit-down place."

"I'll add extensive knowledge of after-church eating habits to the list of things I know to be true about Royal Hewitt."

He cocked his head to the side, a grin forming on his lips. "You're making a list?"

Pink stole across her cheeks. "I do it for everyone I know. Don't get a big head."

"Uh-huh." He winked and set the bag on the floor by his feet as he closed the door and fastened his seatbelt. "All right. Let's get the show on the road."

"You're sure your parents aren't going to mind me staying at their house?" Sophie glanced over her shoulder as she shifted into reverse. "I don't mind getting a hotel."

"They're fine with it." At least, his dad had said it was okay. Royal hadn't been able to run it by his mom. Surely Dad was going to mention it. And if not, they could figure something out then. Maybe head down to Indigo's place tonight instead of tomorrow. "I should probably warn you."

Sophie eased into traffic before looking over. "About?"

"Things with my parents are a little tense right now. In the spring, Skye and I did one of those DNA kits."

"Yeah? I keep thinking about doing one of those. I'd like to get my sister to do one, too—I really think one of us has to be adopted." She laughed. "Given how well I don't fit in, I'm guessing me."

"You laugh."

Sophie covered her mouth and drew in a breath. "Oh my gosh! You found out you were adopted? I'm so sorry. I was kidding. I look too much like my parents to ever think it was a possibility."

"Not quite. But we did find out that there's another Hewitt sibling out there who we hadn't known about." This might be the first time Royal had said it out loud that clearly. He had another sister out there. The whole idea was crazy.

"So . . . how does that work?"

Royal had to give her points for tact. "Turns out Mom and

Dad have this arrangement. Only he wasn't supposed to have any other kids. Mom said she was fine with him needing variety —those are her words—as long as he only had a family with her. Since that didn't end up being what happened, she's ticked. Dad had some big medical issues around the same time as this was all coming out. Like I said, it's tense."

"Maybe I should get a hotel. I don't want to make things awkward."

Royal grabbed the bag of food at his feet and opened it. He handed over a box of fries before partially unwrapping a hamburger and offering it. He dipped into his own fries and chewed. "I don't think your presence is going to make things any more or less awkward. Especially since Skye asked me to have dinner with Jade—that's the new sister—when we're in Phoenix."

"Wait. What?" Sophie frowned as she bit into her burger. "You said we were only going through Phoenix because it was the best place to rent a trailer."

"That's still true. It's just not the whole truth." Royal hunched his shoulders. "I'm sorry. I'm still trying to figure this all out, and I didn't want you to feel like you had to be involved. I figured I could meet her somewhere for dinner, and you could do the room service thing and no harm no foul."

Sophie pressed her lips together. The seconds ticked by in overwhelming silence. Finally she nodded. "I guess I don't blame you. I'm coming with."

He blinked. "Why would you want to do that?"

"Call it curiosity. It's not every day you get to sit in on a meeting between long lost siblings." She shrugged. "Plus, you might need backup."

"I don't think she's an international assassin."

"But that's just what international assassins go for. And serial killers, for that matter. Everyone always says they were quiet, kept to themselves."

Royal laughed and some of the tightness across his shoulders eased. "I'll introduce you as my bodyguard then, shall I?"

"Sure. Why not?" Sophie shook her head. "I thought my family was crazy."

"Sorry. I think everyone's family has quirks."

"To be fair, illegitimate children exceed the term 'quirk.'"

"You're probably right."

"I know I'm right." She grinned over at him before unhooking her phone from the clip on the dashboard. "Here. Choose some tunes. We'll see if you have any taste in music. I reserve the right to revoke your privileges, though, if it turns out you don't."

Royal took her phone and tapped the music streaming app on her home screen. That had to mean it was the one she used most, didn't it? A scroll through her recent listens had the corners of his mouth tipping up. She liked a lot of the same bands he did. He chose one, nodding as the first song came on. "These guys are good. Nice, too."

Sophie took the phone and hooked it back on the clip. "You've met them?"

"Sure. When they put out their first album, they did a lot of low-key social media promo. My rates are pretty accessible, so they reached out. I liked what I heard, did some extra mentions simply because I was a fan. One thing leads to another and we've hung out a few times—if we're in the same place, I always try to reach out. Doesn't always happen, but it can."

"You know they're coming to Albuquerque in January, right?"

"Are they? I hadn't heard."

"Show's already sold out."

"Yeah. They're getting a decent following now."

Sophie glared at him. "You're going to make me beg, aren't you?"

Royal laughed. "Nah. If you're willing to make a date with me almost four months away, I'll see what I can do."

"I didn't say anything about it being a date."

"That's okay. I did."

8

Sophie waited in the guest bedroom until she heard voices and clinking dishes from down the hall. She'd been awake for more than an hour, but the house had been so silent, she hadn't wanted to be the one who broke it. Now that someone else was awake, she gathered her backpack, glanced around the room once more, and headed toward the kitchen.

"Morning, honey." Elise, Royal's mom, turned from the stove to smile at Sophie. "You sleep okay?"

"Yes, ma'am. Thank you."

"It's Elise. Please. Can I get you come coffee?"

"I can get it." Sophie set her backpack against the wall and moved toward the counter. "I thought I heard voices."

"Royal just popped out to the garage for me. He and Martin should be back in soon." Elise stirred eggs in the pan. "I hope scrambled works."

"It's great. Thanks." Sophie wasn't a huge breakfast eater, but she could roll with it. Eggs and toast were easy enough. She poured a mug of coffee and doctored it. "Can I help?"

"If you don't mind making toast, that'd be great." Elise

nodded toward the toaster. Two slices had already popped up. "It's nice of you to drive Royal out."

Sophie took the warm toast and set it on the empty plate by the toaster before putting two slices of bread in and pressing down the lever. She sipped her coffee. "I had some time, and he wasn't sure about driving the trailer."

Elise nodded. "I imagine it's been a while What do you do?"

Here she thought she'd avoided all the chitchat when they arrived close to eight last night. "I'm sort of between everything right now. I'd like to figure a way to make a living with horses, but I don't know how feasible that is."

"It's good to do what you love. All our kids have done that— or, well . . ." Elise trailed off.

Should she say something? Sophie cleared her throat. "Royal mentioned some of what's going on."

"Oh?" Elise paled. "Well. I guess that makes sense."

"What makes sense?" Martin shuffled into the kitchen with Royal on his heels. "Smells good."

Elise sent Martin a fulminating glare. Finally, she said, "Sophie knows all about your other family."

"No. I just—"

"Mom." Royal rested a hand on Sophie's shoulder and squeezed gently. Sophie took it as a show of support. She wasn't sure what else it could be.

"It's not a family. One more kid does not a family make." Martin stabbed a finger in the direction of Elise, his voice a slightly slurred snarl. "But it's nice to know you'll talk about it with someone, since you won't talk about it with me."

"What's there to say?" Elise slammed the spatula down on the stove so hard a piece of the plastic handle broke off and zoomed across the kitchen. "Seriously, Martin. What do you want me to say?"

"Say you understand." Now Martin was yelling. His face turned a dark, nearly purple, red. "We had an agreement."

"Yes. We did." Elise stepped closer, leaning in to Martin's face, fury vibrating off of her. Her voice dropped to a growl. "And you broke it."

Sophie eased back, glancing at the doorway out of the kitchen. She really didn't need to be here for this.

Royal caught her hand. When she looked up, he looked lost. "Stay. Please?"

His anguished whisper twisted her heart. She nodded and took a deep breath. It wasn't as if her parents never fought. They just tended to do it politely and, whenever possible, behind closed doors. When they weren't being passive-aggressive. But, at the end of the day, Sophie always knew they loved her. She wasn't convinced that was the case for Royal.

Martin and Elise were screaming in each other's faces now.

"Hey! Cut it out." Royal took a deep breath and nudged between his parents. "I'm serious. We have company. And this isn't the way to solve things."

"Tell that to him." Elise crossed her arms and turned away.

Smoke curled in tiny wisps from the pan on the stove. Sophie scooted around to turn it off. The eggs were ruined. But that was easier to fix than the rest of it would be.

"Do you think it was easy for me?" Martin took a gulping breath. "I cut all contact when she told me. I sent money when I could, but things were tight, and I knew you'd ask questions."

His color didn't look good. Sophie opened her mouth, but Elise whirled back around and pointed at him. "That's somehow better? Now this poor child grew up without a dad, maybe without the food and clothing she needed because you didn't want to own up to the fact that you'd broken my trust? Don't you try to tell me you did it for me. You did it because you're a coward."

Martin stared, open mouthed, for the space of several heart-beats. He was still beet red. Sweat dripped from his temples. He shook his head. "I'm going for a walk."

"Dad—"

"Leave it alone, Royal. If you have to get on the road before I'm back, it was nice to see you."

Royal bit his lip and took a hesitant step after his father as the man shuffled from the room.

"Let him be." Elise sighed. "He'll walk for hours then come back. Maybe now we'll actually have to talk about it instead of ignoring things."

"Mom."

"Don't. Okay?" Elise turned to Sophie. "I'm so sorry this was your introduction to our family. I hope it doesn't make you less interested in Royal. He's a good catch. A good man. Maybe you could grab breakfast at a drive-through, though. I think I'd like to go lie down."

"I'm not—"

"We aren't—" Royal's eyes were laughing as they met Sophie's.

"Oh. Of course." Elise shook her head. She patted Royal's cheek. "Don't be clueless, baby, okay? Have a safe trip. Give Indigo my love."

Well. That was something. Sophie glanced at Royal. "Are you okay?"

He shook his head. "Not really. But I am sorry you had to be here for that."

"I did try to leave."

He snorted. "I appreciate you staying. Although I'll be honest, I thought it might help diffuse things faster. I'm sorry."

Sophie rubbed his arm. "Should we clean up before we leave? I don't feel right leaving the kitchen like this."

"That'd be good."

Sophie shook the burned eggs out of the skillet into the garbage disposal, flipped on the tap, and looked for the switch that would turn it on.

"It's here." Royal pointed. "Want me to get it?"

"Sure. Thanks." Sophie spun as it whirred to life, and looked around. She'd scrub out the pan and then, "Should we just throw the spatula away?"

Royal flicked the disposal back off and took the spatula. He frowned. "I don't know. Why don't we wash it and let her figure it out."

"All right. I think when the pan's washed, we'll be set. There's toast—do you want to just eat it and hit the road?"

"Why don't I slap on some jam, and we'll take it to go?"

She nodded and rinsed the pan before setting it in the drying rack. With one last look around to be sure there wasn't something—anything—else she could do that might help, Sophie grabbed her backpack.

"Ready?"

Sophie nodded. She'd like to be long gone before Martin got back from his walk. On the positive side, seeing Royal's family drama made her appreciate her family just a little bit more.

SOPHIE DROVE through the gate and stopped, watching in her rearview mirror as Royal swung it closed and made sure the latch was caught.

He hopped back in and shut the truck door. "Okay. According to Indigo's text, it's straight down the road, through the main part of the commune, then a right when there's no other choice."

Sophie laughed, shifted back into Drive, and started down the narrow dirt path. "'Road' is a loose term."

"Yeah. Sorry. Your truck okay?"

"It's a truck." She smiled. "I'm not one of those people who get upset when there's dirt on my tires. There's a reason to drive a truck. Dirt roads are part of that. I guess I just expected more."

"Me, too."

"You haven't been here before?"

Royal shook his head. "Nah. Indigo sent some pictures when she and Wingfeather settled here, but I never felt the need to swing by."

"Wingfeather. He's Native American?"

"He wishes."

"Oh. I thought—"

"Oh yeah, that's what he wants. Indigo feeds it. They do some tribal ceremonies sometimes and he's supposedly in training to be a shaman. But Indigo came across his birth certificate a few years ago. He was born Robert Grissom. At least he didn't lie about his age."

"What about his parents? Hasn't she met them?" Even with an unconventional living arrangement—although was living together and not being married even considered unconventional anymore? Probably not—wouldn't family still be a thing?

"He says they're deceased. Indigo never pushed him on it." Royal shrugged. "Here's the 'town.'"

Sophie nodded as they drove slowly past squat adobe buildings. She caught glimpses of brightly colored fabric waving in the wind behind a couple of the houses—laundry out to dry? Maybe something else. "What kind of commune did you say?"

"They're all artists of some sort. My sister does fiber art— from scratch."

"What's that mean?"

Royal pointed to the right when they approached a dead end. "She has sheep and alpacas. Maybe some llamas. I can never remember. Anyway, she maintains the herds, does the shearing herself, and processes the wool. She sells some of the yarn she spins, but she weaves and knits, too."

"Wow."

"Yeah. She's always been on the go."

That would be her sister. Always moving. Always working. Always winning. Whereas Sophie was so laidback, she had time to take a multi-day trip just so someone she knew didn't have to rent a truck. Maybe it meant Sophie had a generous heart—she'd have to ponder that—but it also probably meant she was as rudderless as her mother accused her of being. "This it?"

Royal nodded. "Looks like. Those are alpacas, right?"

Sophie eyed the funny-looking animals clustered around a mound of hay in the bare pasture to the left. "Think so."

"Oh, there's Indigo. At least I recognize her."

Sophie chuckled and pulled the truck up behind a beat-up station wagon and parked. "Should we have stopped in town for lunch?"

"Nah. I'm sure she has something we can scrounge. You like peanut butter?"

Sophie shrugged. "Sure."

"Come on." Royal grinned and hopped out of the truck. He waved his arm over his head. "Indigo!"

"Hey Royal! Glad you made it. Hungry?" Royal's sister rushed toward him and pulled him into a back-slapping hug. "Who's your friend?"

Royal stepped back and gestured for Sophie to join him. "Sophie, this is my sister, Indigo. Sophie works at the ranch sometimes, teaching kids to ride."

"Cool. Nice to meet you. Come on in—unless you want to tour the paddocks?" Indigo gestured to the animals milling around.

"Alpacas or llamas? Royal couldn't remember."

Indigo frowned at her brother. "Both. Mostly alpacas, though

I have a couple of llamas more for guarding purposes than anything else. I also have Finnsheep."

"Finnsheep?" Sophie looked around. She didn't see any sheep. Let alone sheep with fins.

"They're in the back pasture—it's a breed originally from Finland. Their wool is amazing to spin and work with."

Sophie's cheeks burned even though no one could possibly guess she'd been imagining a cross between sheep and sharks. "Cool."

"You don't knit or anything, do you?"

"Sorry."

Indigo grinned and jerked her head toward the little house. "It's no big deal. I won't bore you with the tour, though. Why don't you come on in? Did you eat?"

"Nope." Royal tucked his hands in his pockets and started up the steps to the house. "I figured you'd have something."

"Of course you did." Indigo rolled her eyes and looked at Sophie. "Do you have little brothers?"

"Little sister."

"Is she as bad as this?"

Sophie thought about her sister—the embodiment of perfection as far as anyone else was concerned. "Maybe worse. In different ways."

"Hey. I'm not that bad. I just know Indigo actually likes cooking." Royal held the door open for them. "But I can head back into town if you'd rather have greasy burgers, Sophie."

The unspoken "again" hung in the air. Sophie ignored her watering mouth.

Indigo made a face. "Yuck. Come on. I made bread this morning and I have some lentil stew from last night."

"Lentils? Ugh. You remember when Mom went through her vegan phase?" Royal made a gagging motion.

"About that." Indigo pointed toward the tiny kitchen where two stools were wedged under a skinny lip of counter.

"Oh man. For real?" Royal sighed.

Sophie looked between the siblings, lost. "I like lentils?"

"They'll be gross. Is this all Wingnut's influence?"

Indigo shook her head. "Wing*feather* was gone when I decided to go all the way. We were close—we'd had some chickens so there were always eggs. But beyond that it was an easy enough move. I do miss butter. I'll own that. The substitutes are not amazing. So I've mostly switched to herbed oil."

"Royal said your husband—"

"Partner." Indigo interrupted Sophie with a smile.

"Right. He's been gone since July? Are the police looking for him?"

Indigo shook her head. "I talked to them, briefly, in August. But since I can't say for certain that he's in danger, and I don't know exactly where he was headed, they opened a file but basically said sometimes people decide to leave. Since we're not really on the grid here, it's unlikely a private investigator would be able to find him. I reached out to the shaman who was guiding his quote-unquote 'spiritual exploration,' but it's been six weeks and I haven't heard back."

"Have you gone out there? Don't you want to know what's going on?" Royal paced from one side of the small kitchen to the other. "It's so cowardly. If he wanted to leave, why wouldn't he say something?"

Indigo took a container out of the fridge and began scooping from it into bowls. "Maybe he didn't know how. It doesn't matter. We were never married, so breaking up is simple. The animals are mine. The house is his. I've been paying the rent, since I want to live here, but we're due to renew the lease in December. I can either transfer it to my name then or . . ."

The silence was broken only by bowls clinking together as

Indigo slid them into the microwave, followed by the beeping buttons.

"Or?" Royal crossed his arms.

Sophie studied him. The protective side of him was something she hadn't seen yet. Was it a good thing?

Indigo turned and leaned against the counter. "Or I could load up the animals and see if the grandparents are as welcoming as everyone says they are."

"You'd do that?" Sophie couldn't fathom the willingness to uproot at the snap of a finger. "Your friends are here. Your whole setup?"

Indigo shrugged. "We grew up moving around. I've been here a while—maybe it's time for a change. There's a guy —Joaquin?"

"Wait. Joaquin at the ranch? That Joaquin?" She didn't know him well—hadn't had many opportunities to interact with him —but if the Hewitts employed him, he was probably a good guy.

Royal nodded. "Yeah. He's cool."

"We've been going back and forth about different types of herds. He really wants to have something livestock-related at the ranch. I could use the help. Finnsheep tend to have multiples. If I'm going to stay here, I need to seriously thin the herd. I can sell some. But I can't guarantee they wouldn't end up on a plate, and I really don't want to do that. I'd have more room, and help, at the ranch. If nothing else, that would buy me time to find fiber homes for any of the animals I need to get rid of." Indigo took the bowls out of the microwave and set them on the counter. She brought spoons over from beside the fridge and gestured for them to go ahead. "I'll get the bread."

"You've been thinking." Royal dipped a spoon into the thick stew and scowled at it.

Sophie scooped up a bite, blew on it and popped it in her mouth. "Mm. This is good."

Indigo laughed. "Thanks for not sounding surprised. Come on, Royal. Try it."

"Fine." He took a bite and chewed. Finally, he nodded. "All right. It's better than anything Mom made."

"See? How is Mom? Have she and Dad figured things out yet?"

Sophie glanced at Royal and their gazes locked. Her appetite evaporated. She really didn't want to get into the family drama again today.

Royal shook his head. "No. I'm not sure they're going to. It came up this morning and we ended up leaving without breakfast."

"Ah." Indigo sawed through a round loaf of crusty bread. "I should go up and try to help. But my neighbors are already sick of helping with the herds. I don't think I can ask them to be completely in charge."

"Don't worry about it. I don't think there's anything we can do." Royal cleared his throat. "I'm, uh, supposed to meet Jade in Phoenix tomorrow."

"Wow." Indigo started laughing.

"What?" Royal reached for a slice of bread, ripped off a piece, and dunked it in the stew.

"Just seems like you chose a strange trip to bring your girl-friend on. But hey, welcome to the Hewitt family, right?"

Sophie met Indigo's searching gaze and her protest died on her lips. "Every family has some kind of drama."

9

Royal was still mulling Sophie's sidestepping of the girlfriend comment the next day. Did that mean she wasn't opposed to the idea? This trip hadn't exactly been romantic. They'd had a lovely date—one where she'd held his hand, even—but since then they'd been back to friends. Although, "friends" was a step up from where they'd been at the start of September.

"You're quiet." Sophie glanced over at him. "You okay?"

"Yeah. It's just a lot. I tried calling my dad, but he's not picking up. I don't know if I should call Mom or just let it be. And as much as I love the idea of Indigo coming to Hope Ranch, I'm also wondering just how that'll work out. I mean, of the kids, she's the one least likely to be interested in Jesus. Will Betsy and Wayne still accept her, even if she never comes to Him?"

Sophie snorted. "Please. Have you met your grandparents? Of course they will. They welcomed you, didn't they?"

They had. And he'd been right where Indigo was—well, maybe not quite as bad off. He hadn't been into the weird "spiritualism" that Indigo dabbled with. "Yeah. That's true."

"Don't stress about Indigo. From what I saw? She's going to

be okay. And Hope Ranch is the best thing that could happen to her." Sophie reached over and rested her hand on his leg. "Call your Mom."

Royal put his hand on top of hers, savoring the comfort and warmth that came with the contact. Maybe they were on their way to being more than friends after all. He grabbed his phone and tapped on the contact for his mom.

"Hi, Royal. Have you heard from your father?"

There was the tiniest hint of worry in his mother's voice. Royal frowned. "No. That's why I was calling. I tried his phone, but he didn't answer."

"He left it here. It's in the garage next to the cot he slept on when you were visiting."

Royal closed his eyes. He'd noticed the cot, but had hoped it was just stored that way. Royal had slept on the couch so Sophie could have the spare room. Dad must normally be sleeping in there. Which meant things between his parents were a whole lot worse than he'd realized. "Have you looked for him?"

"I'm not sure where to start, to be honest. He said he was going for a walk. It's not unusual for him to be gone three or four hours when he does that, but if he's going away for longer, he takes the car."

Maybe they should turn around and head back. Except he'd lose the recording equipment if they did. The seller had already agreed to hold it through tomorrow, and he'd hinted at other interested parties. He fought a groan. "Should we come back and help?"

"No. Don't do that. I'll get in the car and look around. But he probably got a hotel room somewhere."

"You could check the bank statements online, right? That'd show if he did that."

"Sure. If I knew the passwords. Your father handles all of that." His mom sighed. "Maybe after I drive some of his usual routes, I'll drop by the bank and see if they can look it up for me."

"Okay. Let me know, would you? I'm starting to get concerned."

"Royal, your father is a capable adult. Don't stress about him. I'm sure he's fine. He's just being his usual obnoxious self. Honestly, he's been restless since the spring. Once he was back from the hospital and all of you left, he's been taking longer and longer wanders. I wouldn't be surprised if he decided we needed to sell the house after all and get a little camper instead."

"Would you go with him?" He hadn't meant to ask, but the words had tumbled out before he could think twice about them. Royal held his breath as he waited for his mom to answer.

"I guess. I'm not great at being alone, and I kind of feel like I'm too old to try it. As annoyed as I am with him, your father's a known entity. Maybe that's good enough."

Royal looked out the window and tried to gather his thoughts into something coherent. "Do you love him still?"

"I'm not sure I ever did. What does it mean to love someone?" His mom's laugh was tired. "Don't worry about it, Royal. We'll be fine."

"I know Wayne and Betsy left a Bible at the house when they were out in the spring. Maybe if you read that, you'd get a better idea of what love is supposed to be."

"Oh, Royal. Don't you start, too."

"I won't say I'm sorry, but I won't push. I love you, Mom. Go look for Dad. And if you need us to come back, let me know." They said goodbye and Royal ended the call with a sigh.

"Your dad didn't come home?"

Royal shook his head. "If she needs me to come, I can rent a car in Phoenix. I don't need to keep you out here dealing with all this mess."

"I don't have anything better to do right now." Sophie

shrugged. "Let's just take it as it comes. I think we're almost there."

They followed the GPS instructions to get to the hotel and parked. Sophie seemed to understand that he wasn't interested in talking about it. She also didn't seem to feel a need to fill the truck with chatter. She just let him be.

It was relaxing.

When they'd checked in, Royal waited while Sophie went into her room. When her door was closed, he walked down the hall to his own room. It was a standard room, done in the typical gray and beige of business-traveler hotel décor.

Royal dropped his duffel bag on the bed and wandered into the bathroom. Maybe he'd shower before dinner. Indigo had insisted on giving them a tour of the pastures and paddocks that morning, and Royal wasn't convinced that he didn't still smell like sheep. Indigo had been going out to do the morning chores and had wanted the company. Or she hadn't wanted them alone in her house. Either was possible—Indigo could be private.

Still, it was interesting. It was a side of Indigo he wasn't used to, but it fit her.

She'd named all the alpacas after science fiction characters. She called them her space llamas. Even though they weren't all llamas. The sheep all had names, too, though they ran the gamut of popular culture references. How she kept them all straight was a mystery.

Thoughts of Indigo and her animals—as well as the logistics of trying to move it all to Hope Ranch, even though it wasn't his problem—kept him well occupied. There was part of him that knew he was avoiding thinking about his dad. And his mom. And wondering what, if anything, she'd discover.

He sighed and draped the wet towel over the shower curtain. Now that he'd allowed that tiny bit of thought to surface, he was going to have to check in.

He still had an hour before he needed to leave for dinner with Jade. Before *they* needed to leave. So far, Sophie was still planning to join him. Was she just a glutton for punishment?

Royal shook his head. He was glad she was coming—and maybe having her along would keep him from being abrupt. Or rude.

He still didn't want to meet Jade. Let alone have dinner with her.

His mother's phone went to voice mail.

Royal drummed his fingers on his knee before tapping Skye's contact.

"Are you at dinner? On the way?" Skye picked up with a rush of words.

Royal laughed. "I have an hour. Have you heard from Mom?"

"No. Why would I?"

"I just—" Royal paused and scrubbed a hand over his face. "Dad stormed off yesterday morning. Mom hadn't heard from him earlier this afternoon and was going to go look. I'm just worried."

"You know how Dad gets. He's probably at a hotel with room service."

"That's basically what Mom said. He didn't look good, though. And he was so angry. I'm telling you, Skye, I've never seen him this mad."

"Not even when Cyan backed the bus into that light pole?" Skye chuckled.

The memory made Royal smile. Dad had been *ticked*. "Nope. Compared to yesterday, that thing with Cyan was mild irritation."

"Huh." Skye paused, then sighed. "Let me try Mom. You should get ready—you're not bailing on Jade, right?"

Royal glanced down at the dark jeans he'd pulled on after

his shower. "I'm already ready. I even brought a button-down shirt just for this. No tie. I draw the line at a tie."

"I heard you wore a tie for Sophie." Skye's voice had a teasing sing-song to it. "Weren't you ever going to mention you'd gone on a date with her?"

"I hadn't planned on it, no. At least not until I knew if I was going to get to go on a second one. She's coming along to meet Jade. But she's seen so much Hewitt family drama on this trip, I'm not sure it'll count."

"She hasn't pushed you out of the truck and abandoned you on the side of the road. I'd say that's a pretty good sign that she's interested enough in you to stick around and see how things shake out."

"Or she's someone who keeps her word." Royal figured it could go either way. "Look, call Mom, okay? And if you get a hold of her, shoot me a text?"

"Do not check your texts during dinner with Jade!"

"Why not? This is kind of important. It's not like I'm going to be glued to my phone. And if Jade is a modern woman, she ought to be used to it."

"It's rude."

"Yeah, well, extenuating circumstances."

Skye sighed and her breath crackled in his ear. "Fine. On one condition."

"What's that?"

"Pray with me. Right now. Out loud."

Royal closed his eyes. He'd been praying—quietly to himself —since his dad stormed off. He wasn't convinced he was doing it right though. "Skye—"

"I'll start, okay?"

"Yeah, all right." Maybe his sister wasn't the best person to talk to about what prayer was supposed to be. She'd been a Christian longer than him, but she was still Skye. Everything seemed a little easier for her than most people. At least from where he was standing.

His prayer was shorter and more succinct than hers, and as soon as he said "amen," Skye hung up to try and touch base with Mom.

That was fine. Good, even.

He checked the time and grabbed his phone again to text Sophie.

I'M READY. THOUGHT I MIGHT TAKE A WALK UNLESS YOU'RE SET?

Royal hit Send and dug through his duffel for the loafers he'd chucked in to make his outfit a little more presentable for this dinner. It was an awful lot of effort for this person who had caused such a major disruption in their lives.

Skye insisted that knowledge of Jade hadn't caused Dad's aneurysm, but Royal wasn't convinced. And now? Mom and Dad were fighting, Dad had stormed off—and it could all be laid at Jade's feet.

Except maybe Dad was to blame. He'd been the one who went off and started a new family. Jade wasn't responsible for any of that.

She'd just been the one to bring it to light.

A knock at the door interrupted further musing.

Royal slipped his phone into his pocket as he crossed to open it.

Sophie grinned at him. "I'm set. There's never anything good on hotel TVs."

It took a minute for Royal to find his words. She was wearing slacks and a floaty, floral blouse that made her look delicate.

"You okay? Am I underdressed?"

"No. You're good. You look really nice." Royal swallowed and chided himself for being an idiot. "Let me grab my wallet and we can go."

"Heard anything new from your mom?" Sophie leaned against the door to hold it open.

"Skye's going to check in and then text me with an update." Royal slipped his wallet into his pocket and snagged the room key off the dresser.

"During dinner?"

He groaned. "What's wrong with that? It's not like this is a date!"

Sophie's eyebrows lifted but she didn't say anything.

Royal could feel the disapproval pumping off her. "What?"

"Nothing." She gave him an overly bright smile. "Are we walking to the restaurant?"

"Unless you'd rather drive?"

"Walking is good." Sophie started down the hall toward the elevators.

Great. Just great. She was ticked. Skye was ticked. Maybe he could manage to annoy Jade and have a trifecta of women irritated with him. He jogged to catch up just as Sophie jabbed the call button for the elevator with undue force. "Should I tell Skye not to contact me?"

"Do what you want." Sophie stepped into the elevator when the doors slid open.

"Why is it a big deal to get one text? I don't even need to respond. I can just see that she talked to Mom, and Mom told her she found Dad and he's at home, and my world is back to normal instead of the screwed-up mess that it currently is. Except, oh, that's right, that's not going to happen, because even if Dad does go home, it won't change the fact that I have a half-sister that I was never supposed to find out about!" Royal took a deep breath to try and calm the thrumming of blood in his ears.

Sophie bit her lip and eyed him. "Feel better?"

"Not really."

That coaxed a smile out of her and she reached for his hand. "Would waiting until after dinner really be that big of a deal?"

Royal sighed. Probably not. It wasn't like he could go racing back up to his parents' house if Mom hadn't found Dad. And if she had, he'd still be safe after dinner. "I guess not. I'll text Skye and tell her I'll check in after dinner. She'll want to hear about Jade anyway."

Sophie squeezed his hand as they exited the elevator and started toward the front of the hotel. "That's a better idea."

Royal looked at her and some of the jagged edges of nerves smoothed out. "I'm glad you're here."

10

"Surprisingly, I am too." Sophie winked.

Royal laughed. "Way to keep me from getting a big head."

"Someone needs to." Sophie bumped his hip as they walked, their hands still linked. He wasn't what she'd thought. Sure, she still caught little glimpses of the flirty playboy, but now they seemed tamer. Harmless. Royal had told her he'd changed. His behavior seemed to back it up. And yet, was it only attraction between them, or something more?

Sophie could admit the attraction.

But there should be more of a foundation if whatever she and Royal built together was going to last.

"You're quiet." Royal looked up from the map on his phone. "You okay?"

"Yeah. Thinking."

"Dangerous." He winked. "I think we go this way."

Sophie leaned over and looked at the map before nodding. The little blue dot that showed their position was close to the red arrow indicating their destination. "Almost there, looks like. How do you feel?"

"That's such a girl question."

"Well. I am one."

"I've noticed." Royal glanced over and grinned. "You're good at it."

Sophie's cheeks burned. What was the appropriate response? She cleared her throat. Maybe it was time to change the subject. She pointed across the street at the squat building with palm trees rising above it. The white awning surrounding it offered a shady spot to wait during the summer. "Is that the place?"

"Looks like. They're busy even on a Tuesday."

He was right. The parking lot was full of cars and people milled around outside as couples made their way toward the restaurant. "We have a reservation?"

"Yeah. It seemed like the easiest way to make sure we could find each other. Since I have no idea what she looks like."

"You don't . . . seriously? She didn't send a photo? You haven't looked her up on social media?" That was bizarre. It was so easy to find people these days—especially people who wanted to be found. If Sophie had been in Jade's place, she would have connected online with every Hewitt she could find. Especially once Skye returned the contact and there was more information to go on.

Royal shrugged. "I didn't—still don't, if we're being honest— want to do this. Skye nagged me into it. I'm only here to keep Jade from tracking down Mom and Dad and making things worse than they already are."

Things between his parents were definitely bad. Could they get worse? Probably. Love made it much easier to hurt people in ways that would be hard to recover from. That was one reason Sophie tended to run in the other direction whenever it seemed like a possibility. She glanced up at Royal through her eyelashes. Maybe it was time to stop running.

Royal held the door for her. It was dim inside and full of muted conversation and the clink of silverware on china.

Was she underdressed? Maybe she should have packed the skirt she'd worn to dinner with Royal before, but she hadn't wanted to wear it again right away. Even though it was basically the only thing she owned that was close to a dress. Sophie inched closer to Royal as he approached the podium.

"Reservation for Hewitt?"

The woman behind the podium smiled. "Your other party is already here. Right this way."

"She's here already?" Royal whispered to Sophie and shook his head. "Eager much?"

Sophie nudged him with her elbow. "She's probably nervous. Be nice."

"I'm always nice."

Sophie simply snorted.

"What? I am. When have I ever been not nice to you?"

So she couldn't think of something off the top of her head. Didn't mean he was *always* nice. She swallowed her comment as the hostess stopped at a table in the back corner where a woman who looked remarkably similar to Skye was already seated at a small, square table for four.

"Enjoy your meal." The hostess slipped away.

Jade scooted back her chair and started to stand.

"Don't get up." Royal belatedly added a smile to the words. He pulled out a chair for Sophie and only spoke again once everyone was seated. "I'm Royal. You look a lot like my twin sister, Skye."

"I was thinking that." Sophie shifted in her seat. Did everyone feel awkward, or was it just her? "I'm Sophie Ellison, a friend of Royal's."

"You're not a Hewitt?" Jade frowned.

"She's a friend of the family." Royal reached for Sophie's hand under the table. "How was your trip?"

"Seriously? That's your opening salvo?" Jade shook her head and picked up the menu, holding it front of her face.

Sophie's eyebrows lifted and she turned to Royal. Why were they even here, if this was how she was going to be?

Royal shrugged. "Might as well order. We can always get it to go if that's what we need to do."

Jade slapped her menu down on the table and scowled.

Sophie waited for Jade to speak. When she didn't, Sophie cleared her throat. "I'm not sure what you expected. You're obviously unhappy with how things are going, but it'd be good if you could give us a clue here."

Royal squeezed Sophie's hand and shot her a grateful look.

"I expected to meet my family." Jade put emphasis on the last word and sent a pointed look at Sophie. "I thought Skye would be here."

"I know she told you she couldn't make it. I watched her send the email. Things are busy right now for her. She would have liked to come." Royal took a long drink of water. "She's enjoyed your email exchanges."

Something in his tone told Sophie that Royal didn't understand how his sister could be that way. She hoped Jade didn't pick up on it. "What brought you to Arizona?"

"We have a customer here. Normally, I do everything virtually—email, video conferencing—but they've been pushing for an in-person and it seemed like a chance to meet the man who abandoned me. Does he even know I'm in the state?"

"No." Royal leaned in. "And he's not going to until I'm sure you can be polite. You've caused enough trouble already."

"I've caused trouble?" Jade's expression was the picture of disbelief. "My mother—"

"Told my father not to bother coming back around unless he

was prepared to marry her and abandon the rest of us." Royal pointed across the table at Jade. "So don't act like she was some sort of innocent party. She knew Dad had a family. She slept with him anyway. And then, when he wouldn't walk away, she slammed the door in his face. So he honored her wishes."

"Yeah, well, they weren't my wishes. No one asked me." Jade crossed her arms.

"No one asked me, either. Parents usually don't."

Jade eyed Royal and finally blew out a breath. "Fine. Why'd you even come?"

"I didn't want to."

"Royal." Any thought of staying neutral flew out the window at his words. Sophie put her hand on his leg. "This is hard for everyone."

He rubbed the back of his neck. "Yeah. Sorry."

"I guess maybe it's good you're here." Jade sent Sophie a strained smile.

The server appeared beside the table and took their orders.

"You really didn't want to come?" Jade fiddled with the silverware, lining it up and nudging the ends.

"I really didn't. Look, Mom didn't know. She knew Dad had other women—turns out they had some sort of agreement about that."

Sophie wrinkled her nose. "That's . . ."

"Yeah. I don't get it. But I guess that's between them. Anyway, he'd promised no other families. According to him, he was up front with the women about that and did his part to be careful."

Jade looked away.

"What?" Royal reached for his water glass.

Jade sighed. "It sounds like Mom. I have another half-brother. Different dad. I know for sure she set out to get pregnant, hoping for marriage. Didn't work out that time, either."

Sophie closed her eyes as her heart broke for the whole

family. All of them, including Jade, her mom, her brother, and the other man.

"Why not?" Royal leaned back to allow the server to put a fragrant basket of bread on the table and distribute the drinks they'd ordered.

"I guess my mom had a thing for married men. He wasn't going to leave his wife, either."

Sophie winced. What would drive a woman to do that? "I'm sorry."

Jade shrugged. "I guess it finally caught up with her. The cancer she died from—it can be caused by an STI. Mom was never what anyone would call abstinent. She always said sex was a natural expression of feelings and nothing to be ashamed of."

Sophie nodded. It was certainly a common enough viewpoint. Not that she believed it was wrong—it's just that God put guardrails around it. Sex, inside of marriage, *was* a natural expression of feelings and nothing to be ashamed of. Outside of marriage? From what Sophie had observed, at least, it never seemed to bring more than temporary happiness.

"You told Skye you were wondering if there was cancer on both sides of the family—that that was why you did the DNA kit." Royal frowned. "Now you're saying you know the cancer your mom had wasn't genetic?"

"It could be. There's no guarantee, you know? It was such a small possibility that I'd end up getting a match with the kit, it seemed like it might be a laugh." Jade drained her drink and reached for the last piece of bread. "But I didn't think a family that came from the guy my mom told me about would turn out to be a bunch of stuffed shirts."

Sophie could see Royal working hard not to respond. She sent up a quick prayer for peace—for both of them, as she was getting irritated herself. "What were you expecting?"

"I don't know. Not this." Jade scooted her chair back and

stood. "You really won't just give me the old man's contact info? I wouldn't have bothered with this at all if he was online like a normal person."

"It's not a good time. I know he'd like to meet you—but he and Mom need to get their feet back under them first."

Jade snorted. "Whatever. I guess I'll see you around. Thanks for the meal."

"But—" Sophie broke off as Jade strode away. She glanced at Royal. "The food hasn't even come yet."

Royal sighed. "I guess we'll have an extra plate."

"I'm sorry. That was pretty much a disaster."

"Yeah. Skye's going to be mad at me." He rubbed the back of his neck. "I could have handled it better."

"Maybe. Then again, maybe not. I don't get the feeling that Jade actually came here looking for family. She's got a lot of anger." Did she recognize the anger—that sense of unfairness—because of her own feelings toward her sister? "We need to pray for her."

"Yeah." The server appeared with the salads before Royal could say more. She looked with confusion at Jade's empty spot as she put the plates down. Royal held up a hand. "She was called away—could you wrap hers up to go?"

"Sure. You want some extra bread?"

"Yeah, why not. Thank you." Royal looked down at his food.

"Not hungry?" Sophie's stomach twisted uncomfortably, but the salad looked good, and the steak she'd ordered sounded amazing. She didn't want it to go to waste. And it was always going to be better hot than cold.

"I'll be okay. As much as I didn't want to do this, I didn't want it to end that way, either." Royal reached for her hand. "Let's pray and eat. And maybe while we're eating, you can come up with something more fun to talk about."

Sophie closed her eyes and listened to Royal bless the meal

and his half-sister. Her mother always told her that relationships worth having started with a strong foundation of friendship. Then, after being friends for a year or more, love might begin to grow. It looked like this was another situation where Sophie was bound to disappoint her mother.

She wasn't sure if she and Royal were friends.

But she was fairly positive she was falling for him anyway.

11

Royal frowned at the map on his phone. They were in the middle of nowhere. They'd turned off the major road—if it could even be called that—an hour ago. Signal was spotty and neither of them had thought to download the map directly. "I'm not sure this is right."

Sophie growled. "Did you check the instructions the seller sent you?"

"Yes." Royal gritted his teeth and bit back a sarcastic response. According to that, they should see another road up ahead. But, Royal looked up and out the front windshield and all he could see was more gravel road.

"Then let's keep going. Unless you have a better idea?"

"I could try calling him. Again."

"Shoot." Sophie slammed on the brakes as a deer leapt in front of the truck. The back fishtailed and the trailer swung wide, spinning the truck. *Bang!* They slammed into a boulder. Steam hissed from the engine. "Well, that's perfect."

"It could be okay. Maybe it's okay. Are you okay?" Royal glanced at her as he unsnapped his seatbelt and hopped out of the truck.

Sophie nodded. "Are you?"

"Yeah." Royal slid his phone into his back pocket. He swallowed and looked at the crumpled front of the truck before slowly walking around to the other side where Sophie stood staring.

"It's not okay."

"No." He blew out a breath. "No, it isn't. Let's take a deep breath and pause a minute." Royal took out his phone. He'd get a little video of the situation, too. Travel mishaps were always good for some laughs.

"What are you doing?"

"Getting a few seconds of footage. It'll be good for the—"

"What is *wrong* with you?" Sophie wrenched the phone out of his hand, then bobbled it and it slipped out of her grasp.

Royal dove, trying to catch his phone before it slammed into the ground. He missed. The word that slipped out of his mouth was not the benign "shoot" Sophie had used.

Biting his lip, he picked up the phone. The screen was shattered but held in place by the screen protector. Maybe it would be fine? Just a bad screen—but he could be careful. He hit the power button.

Nothing.

He tried the finger print scanner on the back.

Nothing again.

"I'm sorry." Sophie hesitantly stepped forward. "Is it okay?"

Royal took a deep breath and blew it out while looking away from her. Yelling wouldn't solve anything. Being angry at her wasn't going to fix anything either. He couldn't trust his voice though, so he shook his head.

"Do you want to use mine? We could call the guy with the equipment. Maybe he'll have a tow truck suggestion."

"That's a great idea." Royal shot her a bright smile. "Do you have his contact information in your phone?"

"Oh. Right." Sophie looked away. "Could we walk? Do you have any idea how much farther it was supposed to be?"

Did he? He wasn't even sure they were where they were supposed to be. Which is what kicked off this whole mess in the first place. "I don't know. I'm still not convinced we're on the right road."

"Right." Sophie blinked furiously, like she was fighting off tears.

"I'm sorry." He felt small. Small and useless. They needed a plan. "Why don't we see if the truck starts."

Sophie sent him a look full of disbelief.

He hunched his shoulders. "It might."

"Yeah, okay." What were the chances of that? One in what, six gazillion? Sophie stomped to the cab and climbed in.

Royal waited, imagining the truck's engine roaring to life. Spluttering to life? Giving even the vaguest indication that life was possible? He shoved his hands in his pockets and approached Sophie.

Her head was resting on the steering wheel. Tears slipped down her face.

Oh man. Hesitant, Royal walked to the open door and reached out to lightly rub her shoulders. "It's going to be okay. We'll figure this out."

She sat up and swiped at her cheeks. "Sure, it is."

"Let's get your cell and call a tow truck." Should they dial emergency services? It wasn't, technically, an emergency. "Go from there."

"Yeah, okay." Sophie reached for her phone and frowned. It wasn't in the clip on the dashboard. "Um. Can you help me find it?"

"Of course." He hurried to the other side of the truck and felt around on the floorboards. His fingers closed on the phone. "Here. Must have fallen in the impact."

"Yeah." Sophie took the phone and looked it over. "Well, it doesn't seem broken."

Royal watched as she turned it on and opened a web browser. He fought the urge to tell her what to do. Or take her phone and do it himself. She was a smart, capable woman.

"We'll go with tow trucks near me, seem reasonable?"

Royal laughed and climbed into the seat. "Sure. You've got signal?"

"Comes and goes." Sophie tapped on the screen and waited.

Royal angled his head to peek at the screen. It was blank. Not a good sign. He glanced at the top of the phone and saw the empty outline of a triangle where there should have been signal bars. "Maybe we should try walking."

"We could give 9-1-1 a shot. It's not really an emergency. Except it kind of is." Sophie tapped the phone button and punched in the number.

"Anything?"

She ended the attempt to call and shook her head. "Nope."

Royal stared out the cracked windshield. What should they do? They hadn't seen many cars back on the bigger road they'd turned off to get to here. Since they turned, there'd been nothing. Well, nothing but a deer. And that had gone *so* well.

"What do you want to do?" Sophie stared at her phone.

"Let's walk back to the bigger road. Maybe there'll be a car we can flag down. Or better cell signal. Something."

"You don't want to try looking for the next turn?"

"Not really. I can't promise it's going to be there. I don't know what we're supposed to do after that. It just seems like a big gamble. At least at the other road we have the possibility of other people."

"Serial killers."

Royal managed a strained laugh. "Let's hope not."

"I'm just saying. My mom drilled it into me—you never

accept help from someone who isn't police, because they could be a serial killer. Or a rapist. Possibly both." Sophie shrugged and slid out of the driver's seat.

"The only other option is to sit here and pray someone comes by. Someone who also is not one of those oh-so-cheery options your mom described." Royal hopped out and shut the truck door. "What do you want to do?"

"How long is it going to take us to get back to the road? For real. We were driving on this one for what, an hour?"

He nodded. "About that."

"So between thirty and forty miles. That's not super realistic."

Royal pinched the bridge of his nose.

"I mean, realistically, how many miles can you walk in an hour? Four?"

"That's a good clip. I don't know that it's sustainable for more than an hour. Maybe two. It's probably more realistic to say two miles in an hour. Maybe three?" Royal glanced down the road in the direction they'd come. Ten to fifteen hours of walking. And they'd have to stop overnight. They could get in four, maybe five hours, before it started getting too dark to be safe. The last thing they needed was for one of them to get injured.

"You don't remember the instructions at all?" Sophie held her phone up over her head, turning around in circles and jumping occasionally. After a moment, she moved around to the bed of the truck, climbed in, then clambered on top of the cab, holding her phone aloft. "If I could get signal, we could at least look those up again. Right? You could find the listing for the equipment and maybe get in touch with the guy?"

"Sure. But if you could get signal, we could call a tow truck. Or the police." Royal shook his head. "That isn't going to help, you know."

Sophie groaned, shoved her phone into her pocket, and slid

down. "I guess. Why are there still places in America without any cell signal?"

"Look around. Who lives out here?"

"There's a road. There has to be someone. Why didn't this guy meet you in town?"

Royal pointed to the trailer. "It's a lot to haul. And there's still the possibility I could say no."

"No way."

"Well, no. I'm convinced I want it. But he has no reason to trust me. But I also didn't want to just pay for it sight unseen. Where he has it, it's all hooked up, and I can test it out before finalizing the deal. Or I could have. Now he's going to end up selling it to someone else because we missed our appointment."

"Don't blame me. Blame the deer." Sophie crossed her arms and scowled at him.

"I wasn't blaming you." Royal kicked a rock and it skittered across the road. Even if he'd been tempted to, he couldn't promise he would've done a better job avoiding the animal. "I'm just frustrated."

"Yeah. Me, too." Sophie sighed and leaned against the truck. "I don't know what to do."

"I really think our best bet is the main road. Even with all the potential problems." He ticked off reasons on his fingers as he listed them. "We don't know for sure we're on the right road. We're not going to magically get cell signal staying here. We haven't seen another person in close to two hours now. Basically, it seems super unlikely that someone is going to come along and help us. So we're going to have to help ourselves."

Sophie looked like she wanted to argue, but after a minute she nodded. "All right."

"Okay. Do you have flares or something? I feel like we should set something up to warn oncoming traffic. Just in case."

Sophie snorted but pointed to the toolbox in the back of her truck. "There should be an emergency kit in there. I'll write a note and collect up the water bottles that we have."

Food and water. It was good someone had thought about that. They didn't have a lot—turned out Sophie wasn't a fan of road trip snacks. It was a definite check in the minus column, but not a deal breaker. Royal smiled to himself and found the Day-Glo orange triangles in the emergency kit. Nothing else seemed applicable—but maybe they should take what passed for a first aid kit along just in case. At least then they'd have a Band-Aid.

"What else do you want to bring?"

Royal tossed the first aid kit to Sophie. "Is there room for this?"

"Sure. I took out most of the clothes—I didn't figure we'd need them."

"We should probably each have one clean change—we don't want to be stuck with wet clothes. And they'll be layers if it gets cold at night. I have a sweatshirt in my duffel, did you bring anything warm?"

Sophie shook her head. "I didn't think I'd need anything."

"We'll manage." He frowned at the trailer. He'd spent the extra five bucks for a handful of furniture pads. Would they work as blankets? He grabbed two out of the trailer and started rolling them up. "Let's bring these, too."

"Huh. I guess I owe you an apology for making fun of you for getting them." Sophie chewed on her bottom lip. "I don't like leaving the truck unattended."

"I know. I don't know what else to do, though." Royal reached for Sophie's backpack and tucked the blankets inside. He went around the truck and opened the passenger door to get his duffel. Digging through, he grabbed the bare necessities before tossing it on the floor and slamming the door. He added his items to the backpack before shouldering it. There was no point in taking more than one bag. "Ready?"

Sophie hit Lock on the key fob and stuffed it into her pocket. "As I'll ever be."

Sophie's feet were killing her. She clicked on her phone and surreptitiously glanced at the clock before hitting the button again and sliding it back into her pocket. How had it only been ninety minutes?

Royal glanced over at her. "Need a break?"

"No. I'm good. I'm okay." She forced a smile. Her mouth was dry and the idea of a break was like the prospect of Heaven. But stopping wasn't going to get them to the road in any useful amount of time.

"Water?" Royal slowed and started to unsling the backpack.

She held up a hand. "No. We don't have much. We should save it. I really am okay."

"Let me know if that changes. What time is it?"

"Almost four." Sophie sighed. "I'm sorry."

"Why?"

"This is my fault."

"No. It's the deer's fault. And maybe mine. I should've been paying better attention to the map." He sighed. "And then my phone broke and . . . I'm sorry we're in this situation. It's way more than you signed up for when you volunteered to help me get some equipment. This whole trip is way more than you asked for."

"I'm still glad I came."

"Why?" He shot her a shocked look. "What part, exactly, has made you even remotely pleased that you're here instead of back home teaching lessons? Was it when my parents blew up and Dad stormed off and disappeared? Was it meeting my incredibly bitter and abrasive half-sister? Or was it getting hit by a deer and trashing your truck so that we could spend the next ten or so hours hoofing it back toward civilization in hopes of finding someone who can help us?"

Sophie snorted out a laugh. "It's been a busy couple of days, hasn't it?"

"It has." He sighed and hitched the backpack straps up. "And I'm frustrated that neither my mom nor Skye seem to feel like it's a problem that he's still gone."

Sophie didn't understand that, either. Hesitant, she reached for Royal's hand and laced her fingers through his. "I'm sorry. I guess it's good, at least, that the bank said he'd pulled out cash yesterday morning."

"I guess."

They trudged on in silence for several minutes. It was pretty —not all that different from the area of New Mexico where Hope Ranch was located. Not completely the same, either. But birds were singing in the forest on either side of the road. Other animals rustled in the ground cover.

Sophie tried to concentrate on anything other than the feel of Royal's hand in hers. What was it about him? Even as frustrating as this current situation was, she couldn't think of anyone she'd rather be stuck with. And that was startling.

How had her opinion of him changed so dramatically in three days? She supposed she'd have to admit it had been changing before that—but now, where she would have been hard-pressed to agree they had a friendship before heading out on this road trip, he was rapidly sliding into the position of best friend.

With potential for more.

If she didn't mess it up.

She sighed.

Her mother would have plenty to say about it. It wasn't like Royal had any sort of traditional employment. As derisive as her mom got about Sophie's desire to have a stable, she could only imagine the mocking Royal would be in for. And then the eternal comparison—and falling short—with her sister. Maybe it was better to walk away before anything happened.

Royal didn't deserve this.

He could do better.

She sighed again.

"What's wrong?"

Sophie stopped and pulled her phone out. She clicked the button to check the screen. "Still no signal."

Royal shrugged out of the backpack and unzipped it. He dug around until he found one of the water bottles. He took a small sip and offered it. "Here."

"Thanks." Sophie stretched her arm above her head and moved the phone around. Why wasn't there signal? Shoulders slumping, she put the phone away and reached for the water.

Royal watched her with a tiny frown. "You're not okay."

It was a statement, not a question. Sophie really didn't want to get into it. She should. She should tell Royal all the reasons nothing could ever work between them long term. He thought his family was strange and dysfunctional, but compared to hers? Even with his parents' odd relationship, they were better than hers. And at least his siblings all got along—they actually seemed to even love each other. What would that be like?

"I'm just getting into my own head." Sophie tried to smile.

"Happens sometimes. I'd suggest we could play some music, but I don't actually have any downloaded to my phone. I just stream. And, well, no signal."

"Plus there's the battery situation. If we do manage to get signal, it'd be good to have enough juice left to call for a tow."

"Right. Good point." She should stop obsessively checking the time, too. Everyone who was surprised she was messing this up, raise their hand. She let out a sardonic laugh that ended in a sigh. "Should we keep going?"

"Take another sip of that." Something in his expression suggested he was considering pushing about what was bothering her. She really hoped he wouldn't. As much as she should call off whatever was happening between them, she didn't want to.

Sophie took a sip, screwed the cap on, and handed it back. "Do you want me to take a turn with the backpack?"

"I've got it." Royal adjusted the straps and wiggled to get it resettled. "I figure we should try to keep going until it gets dark. That work for you?"

"Yeah, I guess. I'd be lying if I said I wanted to walk that long, but I get that we need to." Sophie glanced back over her shoulder at the road they'd already traveled. "I've never been big on science fiction, but I could go for a transporter thing right about now."

Royal chuckled. "Or one of their communication devices that just worked. Everywhere they went, it worked fine. That'd be good, too."

Sophie fell into step beside Royal and nodded. "But if we had the transport thing, we wouldn't have been driving anyway. We could have—what'd they call it?"

"Beamed? I think it's beamed."

"That's right. Beamed over to see the equipment and then right back home."

"Of course, then you wouldn't have needed to come." Royal looked over at her and took her hand. "And I have to say, I would have missed out."

Sophie squeezed his fingers as warmth spread through her at his words. She should back away. She should do it now, before things got any more complicated, but she wasn't going to. She'd just have to deal with it when she messed it up. If she ended up heartbroken? It wouldn't be the first time. "Me, too."

EVERY MUSCLE in her body ached. That was the first thing Sophie noticed when she woke. She was also warm. And there was something warmer and heavy wrapped around her. She shifted slightly and pried her eyes open.

Pine needles. Why was all she could see above her pine needles?

Oh, right.

The events of yesterday came rushing back and she identified a rock poking her hip. Sophie looked down to see Royal's arm around her waist. Which meant she was warm because— she glanced over her shoulder— Royal was snuggled against her back.

The furniture pads had been surprisingly good blankets. Though it would have been nice to have more of them along for extra padding between her and the ground. As much as Sophie enjoyed the outdoors—horseback riding, hikes, even the occasional kayaking trip when people wanted to make the drive to do it—camping was not her thing. Especially not camping without the comforts of a tent, sleeping bag, and air mattress.

Gingerly, Sophie eased away from Royal, careful to cushion his arm so it didn't fall and wake him. There was a nip in the morning air once she was away from the blanket, but she was wearing enough layers that it wasn't too bad.

And she needed to get some distance between her and Royal.

They hadn't started out snuggled together. Who had moved?

She frowned as she looked at him and tried to remember where they each had been when they'd said good night. Maybe they'd both moved.

Her stomach growled.

She'd kill for coffee.

She might as well wish for pancakes, bacon, and eggs to go with it.

Trying to be as careful and quiet as she could, Sophie wandered deeper into some trees to take care of the inelegant process of going to the bathroom in the wild. At least their low supply of food and water meant she didn't have to do it very often.

Finished, she headed back to their makeshift camp near the side of the road. Royal was still sleeping. How?

Sophie powered her phone back up so she could check the time. The sun was up, so they might as well start their plodding toward the more major road. If they started soon, they ought to be able to get there around lunchtime.

She knelt on the blankets and gave Royal's shoulder a little nudge.

Nothing.

She shook his shoulder a little harder. "Royal? We should get up."

"Mmm. 'Kay. Jus' a minute." His voice was slurred, sleepy. His hand slid up her leg and hip to her waist. "Or we can stay here."

"Royal." Sophie wasn't sure what to do with all the nerve

endings in her body firing at once. She gave his shoulder another wiggle. "Come on. Wake up."

"Don't wanna." His eyes cracked open and his smile shot straight to her heart. "Morning."

"Hi." It was a stupid response, but Sophie had only the slipperiest grasp on her language skills, so she went with it.

Royal pushed himself up and stretched his arms above his head. His shoulders popped. He rolled his head on his neck and sighed as he scooted away. "Sorry. I'm just sorry."

Her mouth was dry. She shook her head. It was fine. She couldn't make the words form though.

"I hate camping."

Sophie laughed and the tension dissipated. "Me, too."

"I knew I liked you." He reached up and traced a finger down the side of her face. "How'd you sleep?"

"Um." Her thoughts scattered. She met and held his gaze.

His lips quirked up at the corners. "Sophie?"

What was he asking? She leaned forward. It wasn't a conscious decision, but Royal didn't hesitate. He drew her closer, and his lips whispered over hers once. Twice. The third time they lingered, the kiss strengthening, deepening.

Sophie's eyes fluttered closed. What *was* this? She'd kissed men before. But this? It was the difference between a Kindergarten art project and a Degas.

Royal leaned back, his hands still framing her face. "Wow. Good morning again."

"How'd you sleep?" Sophie scooted away. This was ridiculous. Ridiculous and irresponsible. Ridiculous, irresponsible, and irresistible.

He grinned. "That was my line."

What? Oh. Heat seared her cheeks. "Right. I think you covered it when you mentioned hating camping."

"Yeah. I might end up with bruises." He stretched again and stood. "I, uh, need to . . ."

"Go for it. I'll start breaking camp." Such as it was. She waited until Royal had stumbled into the trees before blowing out a breath and touching her lips. He was a player. Or had been. So it made sense that he could kiss. But man, if there were competitions for kissing, he'd be sure to bring home the gold.

Sophie stood and shook out the blankets before rolling them up as small as she could. She dug through the backpack—a considerably easier task this morning as they'd both pulled on their extra shirts for sleeping—and set out the meager food supplies.

There wasn't going to be a breakfast of champions today.

She was stuffing the blankets on the bottom of the bag when Royal came back to camp.

"What can I do to help?" His hands were tucked in his pockets and the way he stood, did he feel awkward?

"Maybe figure out what we can afford to have for breakfast. There's some trail mix and half a bag of chips. Nothing amazingly healthy."

"Yeah, I'm going to be rethinking my road trip food in the future." Royal squatted beside her and touched her knee. "Should I apologize?"

"No." Sophie set the bag down and turned to look at him. "No, I was in that as much as you were. And I know how to say no."

He studied her for a minute before nodding. "Okay. I'll just put it out there that I'd really like to do it again sometime. Maybe more than once."

Sophie smiled. "We'll have to see what we can do. For now, we should start walking. I don't want to spend another night sleeping on rocks."

"I can get behind that." He reached for the backpack. "Let's go crazy and finish the trail mix. We'll save the chips for a snack."

Sophie checked her phone for a signal one more time before offering Royal her hand. "Shall we?"

He threaded his fingers through hers and squeezed. "Let's pray before we get going."

Sophie listened as Royal quietly asked God to guide and protect them on their walk—and in their relationship.

Their relationship.

Sophie fell into step beside Royal as they walked together toward their future.

13

Royal took what felt like his first deep breath in three days as Sophie turned onto the driveway to Hope Ranch. Home.

He glanced over at Sophie and his lips curved. She was a big part of that feeling of home now, too.

"You're staring."

"I'm not. I'm admiring."

She snorted and angled the truck onto the dirt road that would take them around the main house to Royal's cabin behind it. "Anything from your mom?"

"A couple of texts." The relief he'd felt at being home drained away. Dad was back in the hospital. Mom had finally found him—or, more to the point, the hospital had called her when he'd been brought in. "No change. The machines are doing all the work for him and she's trying to decide what to do."

"I'm still confused why she didn't want you to come back. Shouldn't you be there? All of you?" Sophie reached over and touched his arm before shifting into Park. "I would have been happy to bring you back there."

"That's Mom." Royal shrugged. In some families, maybe, when their mother said not to bother it was a guilt tactic to get you to come anyway. Not his mother. When Mom said no, you went along with it. "It just would've made things worse."

"I'm sorry."

Royal leaned over and brushed a kiss across her cheek. "Thanks. I'll go unhitch the trailer. I can borrow one of Grand-dad's trucks to get it back into town to the rental place after I unload it."

"I don't mind helping."

"You don't need to get home? I've taken up so much more of your time than we planned." He pushed open the door. "I don't want you to feel obligated."

"Royal." Sophie frowned. "Are you upset with me?"

He closed his eyes. "No."

"What's wrong?"

He didn't know how to put it into words. It was a mixture of the stuff with Dad, worry for Mom, and exhaustion. "It's not you. It's just—I'm probably just tired."

She paused, then nodded. "I'm a little tired, too. It hasn't been a particularly restful week. Let's get your equipment unloaded and then you can nap."

"I'm still amazed we were able to get it." Royal unlocked the trailer and pulled open the doors. The recording studio—because it really was an almost complete studio setup—was carefully packed in the space. He reached in and grabbed one of the boxes. "We can just put it in the living room. I'll deal with it later."

"Okay." Sophie reached into the trailer and hefted a panel of soundproofing.

"Hey, you're back." Cyan strolled off the path from the main house and came to look in the trailer. He let out a low whistle. "Nice."

Royal nodded. "Feel free to grab a box and make yourself useful."

Cyan chuckled. "How was the trip?"

Sophie snickered.

"We got the equipment and made it home. I'll call it a win." Royal pushed open the door to his cabin and smiled in spite of himself. Definitely home. "Just set it anywhere."

"It's six extra steps to the spare bedroom." Sophie sidled past him. "We can at least put it where it goes. You can set it up later."

Cyan nodded and followed her. "I agree. Come on. You'll thank us later."

The three of them made quick work of unloading the truck. It was good to have Cyan's help—the man selling the equipment had helped with loading the heavier pieces and Royal wasn't excited about trying to do it with just him and Sophie. She was game, he'd give her that, and they probably would have managed, but his brother was an easier option.

"So. I guess I'll see you around?" Sophie pressed her lips together, her expression full of uncertainty, and glanced at Royal. "I'll turn the trailer in."

Royal walked closer and pulled her into his arms. He rested his cheek on the top of her head for several seconds. "Thanks. I'll call you later, okay?"

Sophie pressed her lips to his. It was brief, but potent. "Okay. I'll talk to you then. Bye, Cyan."

She climbed into the still-banged-up but running truck and started the engine.

"Well, well, well." Cyan slung his arm around Royal's shoulders.

Royal fought the urge to hunch. "What?"

"She's a nice girl."

Was there censure in his brother's voice? "So? What? I don't get a nice girl? I don't deserve someone, too?"

Cyan held up his hands. "I didn't say that. Any of it. Don't get touchy."

"Yeah, well. You could be right."

"I could be . . . but I didn't say it. So I couldn't be right. And if you're honestly thinking that? You're even dumber than I always knew you were."

Royal bristled. He knew his brother was pushing his buttons, but he couldn't stop the response. "I'm not dumb. You're dumb."

Cyan laughed and danced out of reach. "Wanna fight?"

"Jerk." Royal crossed his arms, but a smile tugged at his lips. He sighed. "I guess I'm not sure what she sees in me."

"She probably sees what the rest of us do. Don't let your vision problem ruin it, man." Cyan gave Royal's shoulder a light punch. "Mom was freaked out when you disappeared for two days. With Dad gone, it wasn't the best timing."

"I'll be sure to take that up with the deer that ran us off the road in the middle of nowhere." Royal ran a hand through his hair. "If I never have to walk thirty miles again, I'll be happy."

"That's what happened to the truck?" Cyan shook his head. "Let's go to the grandparents' and get you a drink. Then you can sit down and fill me in. Mom's summary was, and I quote, they had some car trouble."

Royal laughed and fell into step beside his brother as they crossed to and entered the main house. "That sounds like Mom. Yeah, all right. You think they have root beer?"

"Most likely. Maria's started stocking more soda in the main house to keep it away from Calvin." Cyan shook his head. "Like the kid doesn't know he just has to go hit up Betsy to get some."

"Ooh. Bad for him though, right?"

"He'll drink the diet, so it's not really any worse than it is for anyone. I think she's worried less about his blood sugar than the chemicals. She started reading some healthy eating blog—and don't get me wrong, I'm all for eating healthy, so I don't mind that—but it's gotten a little out of hand. She keeps talking about going vegetarian—or even maybe vegan."

Royal wrinkled his nose. "Put her in touch with Indigo. Did you know she's vegan?"

"No. But I guess I'm not shocked." Cyan sighed. "I'll mention it. I'm trying to appear supportive."

"Is that different than actually being supportive?" Royal reached for the handle of the fridge in his grandparents' kitchen.

"It's the first step." Cyan grinned and snaked his arm around Royal to snag a can of ginger ale.

Royal laughed and rummaged around until he saw the root beer. "It's all diet?"

"Makes it easier."

He sighed. "Guess I'll be stocking my own when I finally get settled."

"Your choice." Cyan sat and propped his feet on the coffee table. "So spill it. Your equipment pickup was obviously more fraught than Mom let on."

"Maybe I shaded some of the details for her, when I finally got a new phone." Royal popped the tab on his drink and took a couple of swallows. He related the story, starting from when he began to think they weren't on the right road, the deer, and the endless hike to the main road. "We finally got a cell signal when we were about five miles from the bigger road. Sophie looked up a towing company and got them started toward us, then I was able to call the guy I bought the equipment from. He was ticked —but got over it when I explained. Long story short, even without the deer we were on the wrong road. Anyway, I barely caught him before he relisted it, so that worked out. It all worked out. It just didn't go the way I would've planned."

"What in life does?"

Royal knew Cyan wasn't being glib, but until recently—until

he'd started trying to listen for God's leading in his life—Royal would have said ninety percent of his life went precisely the way he planned it.

"So. You and Sophie?"

"Working on it. I like her."

"I got that." Cyan chuckled. "Seems as though she likes you back. You're not going to break her heart, are you?"

"Not if I can help it."

BETSY LEANED FORWARD as the post-service music began, and looked across Royal to Sophie with a smile. "Can you join us for lunch?"

"I can't. I appreciate the offer. In fact," Sophie winced and looked at Royal, "I'm supposed to see if you're available to join our family."

"Sure. That's okay, right Grandma?" Royal glanced at Betsy. "Maria always plans for everyone, but leftovers aren't a bad thing."

"It's just fine." Betsy patted his knee and stood. "You two have a lovely afternoon."

"I'm sorry. I didn't mean to spring it on you, but my mom cornered me before the service. I guess word got back to her somehow." Sophie sighed. "I appreciate it."

"Did you not want her to find out we were together?" Royal took her hand. They were together. They hadn't sat down and officially declared their undying love or anything, but those kisses—those didn't happen if people weren't together. Did they? Well. In his past they would have, sure. But Sophie wasn't like that. And neither was he. Not anymore.

"It's not that. It's just—I—you know what? You'll figure it out at lunch." Sophie pushed herself to her feet. "Maybe if we're lucky, we can eat and leave."

"And then?" He wanted to spend more time with her. But he also wasn't going to push. If she needed space, he could try and give it to her. He had plenty to do to get his recording studio set up.

She peeked up at him through her eyelashes. "Maybe we could go for a ride?"

"I'd like that." Royal's shoulders relaxed. She wasn't trying to shake him loose. "Let's go eat. I'm starved."

"I'm not sure—you know what, never mind. Come on. We don't want to be late." Sophie tugged his hand.

Royal followed her down the aisle and out into the parking lot. Sophie was adept at skirting clumps of people she knew. Several had eyed their clasped hands and tried to intersect, but Sophie had just given a quick nod, maybe a few words, and they were off again. It was impressive.

The drive from church to her parents' house wasn't long.

The closer they got, the quieter Sophie became.

"Should I have said no? Made up a reason not to come?" He was ready to meet her parents. He was ready to have a conversation about their relationship and where it was headed. But maybe she wasn't. He didn't want to push—or he didn't want to push too hard. That was closer to the truth. Seemed like Sophie could use a little nudge in a lot of areas of her life.

"No. They would have forced the issue sooner or later. It's better to look like you're going willingly."

"The way you say that makes it sound like I'm heading to the gallows."

Sophie shrugged.

"That doesn't inspire confidence."

"They won't kill you. I don't think they're going to like you, but that's nothing new. They don't really like me."

There was a lot in that statement that needed to be unpacked. Now wasn't the time. "Parents love me."

She glanced over and snorted. "I bet they do. Usually. Mine won't. Or, if they do? They'll try to convince you to be with my sister. Except she has a boyfriend—practically a fiancé—and they adore him."

"I suspect you're projecting." Royal reached over and rubbed her leg. "It's going to be fine. When's the last time you brought a guy home for Sunday lunch?"

"Not since high school—sophomore year. So what's that, seven years?"

"Something like that." It was Royal's turn to shrug. "It's going to be fine. More than fine. Like I said, parents love me."

Sophie parked her still-crumpled truck behind a small, gleaming sports car at the curb in front of her parents' house. "Let's hope so. That's my sister's car. So you're walking into a full house. You sure you're ready for this?"

"I am." He frowned as he studied her. For just an instant, worry had been evident on her face. Now she was expressionless and her eyes were flat. "You should play poker."

"Trust me. You learn to keep it all under wraps." She pushed open her door and hopped out of the truck. "Come on. Let's go face the music."

Her parents couldn't be the monsters she made them out to be, could they? He'd had a stray qualm or two about introducing Sophie to his folks—his family wasn't exactly traditional—but he'd also known that for all their faults, Mom and Dad were going to welcome her warmly. If only as a guest. If they'd known —or suspected—the feelings that were growing in his heart? They would have rolled out the red carpet.

Royal reached for Sophie's hand as they walked up the path to the front door.

She gave a little head shake and tucked her hands in her pockets.

Okay, then.

Sophie knocked on the door before pushing it open and calling out. "Mom? Dad? We're here."

"In the kitchen, honey."

"Oh, yay." Sophie muttered it under her breath but jerked her head toward the back of the house before setting off.

Royal followed behind. He'd be lying if he didn't admit he was starting to be a little . . . he'd call it concerned. Were they secretly axe murderers or something?

Sophie kissed her mom's cheek and lifted a hand in greeting to her dad as she entered the kitchen.

Her mom smiled and turned back to the pots on the stove.

"Hi, hon." Her dad grinned and kicked out a chair at the kitchen table. His eyebrows lifted.

"Mom, Dad. This is Royal Hewitt. Royal, my parents."

Royal smiled and, since he was closer, stuck out his hand toward Sophie's dad. "Mr. and Mrs. Ellison, it's nice to meet you."

Sophie's dad shook his hand.

Her mom wiped her hands on a towel before stepping closer to the table to also shake his hand. "I'd love to say we've heard so much about you, but Sophie's a vault, apparently."

"Mom."

Royal smiled and gently touched Sophie's elbow. "I'm happy to answer any questions you have."

"Have a seat." Sophie's dad gestured to the chair he'd pushed out. "You, too, Soph."

"Where's Karla? And I assume Jamie's with her?"

"They went for a little walk. It's so nice to see your sister happy and in love." Her mom smiled as she returned to the stove. "They should be back in the next few minutes. I told them when lunch would be ready."

With a sigh, Sophie sat.

Royal scooted another chair closer to Sophie and sat beside her. Under the table, he reached for her hand and squeezed her fingers. Would she understand he meant it as support? And to remind her that he wasn't worried about this?

"So, Royal." Sophie's dad leaned forward. "What do you do for a living?"

14

Sophie closed her eyes. Leave it to Dad to dive right in.

"Dad."

"What? I can't make small talk?" Dad shot her an innocent look.

Royal touched her leg again. Did he have any idea what he was doing to her? She shifted her gaze to look at him. Probably not. He probably had a lot more experience with that kind of physical interaction. She needed to grow up and ignore it. There was more to life—more to a *relationship*—than the tingles. But oh, boy, were there tingles.

"It's a good question. I do a variety of things that a lot of people consider non-traditional. I'm not sure how well you know my grandparents?"

"Just in passing. They're good people."

Royal beamed. "They are. I'm grateful to finally have gotten to know them—they're so much more, so much better, than my dad ever led us to believe."

"Mmm." Sophie's mom glanced over. "I remember your father. Handsome as homemade sin, and full of himself with it.

He never did appreciate your grandparents. He just seemed determined to rebel, no matter what they did."

"That sounds about right. I'm not my father, Mrs. Ellison. I can promise you that."

Sophie watched her mom digest Royal's words and give a slight nod. Well. That was unexpected. Mom wasn't one to take anyone at face value.

"Anyway. My parents, for all their faults, raised us to do what we love—"

Dad snorted.

Sophie winced. Hadn't Royal listened at all when she was talking?

"Oh, I know. But they gave me the courage to try. And I've made a living—a decent one—doing that. I'm planning on adding voiceover and book narration to my résumé soon. There's good money in that, without the necessity of sponsorships." Royal's smile rivaled that of a car salesman. "I'm starting to realize the strings that come with money aren't always worthwhile."

Sophie struggled not to grin. He had been listening. At least when she'd vented about her parents and the strings they put on their financial assistance. Of course, if she could just live up to their standards, maybe it wouldn't chafe like it did. But experience had taught Sophie that she'd never measure up. It was time to find a way to stop caring.

Dad opened his mouth, but before he could speak, Karla's voice called out. "We're back! Did Sophie finally get here?"

Sophie bristled. "You saw my truck. I'm guessing you figured that out."

"Now, Sophie." Mom turned and shot her a quelling look.

"Relax," Royal whispered. "Don't play her game. She knows just how to push your buttons, doesn't she?"

Sophie frowned. Was Karla doing it on purpose? Egging her

on so Sophie would respond and make herself look bad? She took a deep breath and swiveled in her seat as Karla and Jamie came into the kitchen. Their faces were rosy and glowing—they looked like they'd just stepped out of a particularly windy photo shoot for some preppy clothing catalog.

"Hi, I'm Royal Hewitt. It's nice to meet you. Karla, right? And you're Jamie?" Royal shook hands with each of them in turn. "Your mom was nice enough to invite me for lunch after church."

Karla hesitated before smiling. "It's a good day for it. We have news!"

Sophie swallowed as her gaze darted to her sister's left hand. A rock the size of Gibraltar gleamed on the appropriate finger.

"Oh! At last!" Mom hurried away from the stove, grabbing Karla's hand and exclaiming over the ring before dragging Karla and Jamie into a hug.

Dad stood and clapped Jamie on the back while kissing Karla's head. "Congratulations, sweetie."

"You should see this, Sophie. It's just beautiful. Oh, we couldn't be happier. I wish I'd made something more special for lunch." Her mom flitted back into the kitchen, twisting her hands.

Sophie's smile felt tight. She stood and made what she hoped were the appropriate noises at her sister's ring.

"I'm thinking June. I know it's a cliché, but I just want to be a June bride." Karla giggled and fluttered her eyelashes at Jamie.

"Is nine months long enough to plan a wedding?" Sophie couldn't stop the words—though she didn't try too hard. She hadn't, technically, said anything wrong. But the implication was catty. She knew it.

Royal hid a smile and poked her with his elbow.

"Of course. It's plenty of time. We'll start planning after we eat. Why don't you see if your parents can join us for dessert, Jamie?"

"Oh. Well, Mrs. Ellison, I'm sorry. I told them we'd come by after lunch—they knew, of course, that I was planning to propose. So why don't I talk to Mom, and maybe the three of you ladies can make time this week to get the ball rolling?" Jamie's delivery was smooth—as always.

Karla beamed up at him like he'd said something amazing.

Even Mom gushed about what a good idea it was.

Sophie's stomach twisted. Ugh. It was all just so much.

"Sophie, honey, why don't you set the table in the dining room? Then we can eat." Mom looked up from loading serving bowls to nod toward the formal room that they rarely ate in.

"Really?"

"It's a big day. Use the good dishes, out of the china cabinet." Mom pointed.

"Come on Karla. You can help." Sophie stood and marched toward the dining room. She'd known this was coming. Why did it feel like another example of her inability to ever be enough?

"Oh, no. Karla honey, you sit. I'm sure your sister can handle it. It's your special day."

Sophie stopped. "Mom—"

"I'll help." Royal jumped up and winked at Sophie. "But you'll have to make sure I put the silverware in the right place. My folks weren't big on formal dining rules."

"Royal. You're a guest. You should sit and let my sister—"

"Hey. It's okay." He rubbed Sophie's shoulder. "I'd rather stick with you, anyway."

Royal dragged her by the hand into the dining room, and then pulled her into a hug. She sagged against him.

"I'm sorry. I don't know why this is so hard."

"Because they're making it hard, and you're used to letting

them. Your sister, I think, wants to break the animosity just as much as you do."

Sophie snorted. "She's got an interesting way of showing it."

"She doesn't know how. Not without calling out your folks, too, and she's too cowed by them to do that."

"Cowed? Please. She has them wrapped around her fingers."

Royal shrugged. "Not what I'm seeing. It's always easier to go along than to try and make a change. But I'm new here, I could be wrong. Now—show me the silverware."

Sophie chewed on her lip a moment before pulling out the drawer of the china cabinet where they stored the fancy flatware.

Before long, they'd set the table and everyone was seated. Sophie watched her sister, trying to see what Royal saw. She listened, and for the first time in a long time, tried not to take it personally.

Maybe—just maybe—Royal had a point.

She hoped he'd stick around long enough for her to be sure.

About a lot of things.

SOPHIE FLICKED the brush down the side of Blaze. The stables were quiet—or as quiet as they ever got with stalls full of horses. Usually, she'd run into Morgan when she was in and out. For that matter, Tommy and Joaquin weren't usually as scarce as they had been today. Where was everyone?

She finished grooming the horse and checked that the stall door latched behind her. She'd wipe down the tack and put it back and then? She sighed. She could only put off her job search for so long. She just kept hoping God would take pity and send a clear, recognizable sign. She was praying about it. A lot more than she'd ever prayed about things in the past. And still nothing.

Hands in her pockets, she ambled away from the stable toward the main house. Royal hadn't been in his cabin when she stopped by on the way to ride. Should she try again? He wasn't answering her texts, either.

Maybe lunch with her folks had been too much after all.

Or, he was busy and his world didn't revolve around Sophie. That was a possibility, too. She gave herself a firm mental shake. She shouldn't assume the worst when there were any number of perfectly good other explanations.

She took the side path over to Royal's cabin and knocked smartly on the door. She waited a few seconds before knocking again.

"He's not there." Maria smiled as she stepped out the Hewitt's back door.

"Oh?" Sophie turned and fought her sinking stomach. "Where'd he go?"

Maria frowned. "He said he was going to call you—they all left. All the Hewitts, at least. Martin died."

Martin. Royal's dad. Sophie sank onto the stump that sat beside the door of Royal's cabin. "Oh, boy. When?"

"They got the call late last night. Everyone packed a bag and piled into the trucks." Maria rubbed her eyes. "Cyan drove Skye and Royal. Wayne and Betsy took their own truck. They weren't sure if they'd be welcome, but they wanted to try."

"You didn't go?" That made very little sense. This was her father-in-law. Didn't Cyan want her there?

"Elise said family only. And she made it clear she meant those who shared DNA." Maria shrugged. "I won't lie and say it doesn't hurt, but I'm also not sure I would've wanted Calvin to have his first experience with his grandmother be at the funeral for his grandfather."

That wasn't something Sophie had considered. At the same time, she thought it was great that Maria considered Cyan's parents as grandparents. Sophie didn't know much about step-families, but it seemed like Maria and Cyan were making a good one. "Do you think they told Jade—the new half-sister?"

"Doubt it. Unless Skye did. Skye is still holding on to hope that they'll all make one big, happy family down the line." Maria's lips thinned. "From what I heard Royal telling Cyan, we're better off without that happening."

"That's my first instinct—but she's not a happy person. Maybe she just needs someone—or a whole bunch of someones —to love her." Sophie sighed. Then again, loving people didn't always translate into being treated better. Look at Karla and her parents. "I can't say I loved having dinner with her, but I still feel sorry for her."

"I guess. I wish everyone was easy to love."

Sophie laughed. "Yeah, well, then everyone would do it and it probably wouldn't mean as much."

"There's that." Maria drummed her fingers on her thigh. "Can you stay for lunch? I'm still feeding the guys and there's plenty."

"You wouldn't mind?"

"Not at all. Come on. I'll fix us some tea and we can kick back until they show up."

Tea sounded good. It wasn't like she had anything else to do. And while Sophie didn't know Maria super well, she wouldn't mind making a friend.

"I heard you're having some job troubles."

Sophie's cheeks heated. She wanted to deny it—or demand to know where she'd heard that, but the ranch was like a small town and word traveled. When she factored in all the couples— Morgan and Skye, Cyan and Maria, it wasn't a huge stretch to see how information had spread. "Yeah."

"Do you know what you're looking for?" Maria led the way back into the house.

Sophie shook her head and settled on one of the stools at the counter. "That's part of the problem. I was convinced I wanted this master's—then I'd get a job as an OT with a specialty in hippotherapy and life would be amazing."

"So what happened?" Maria plugged in the electric kettle and took two mugs out of the cabinet.

"Basically, it became super clear that the therapy office in town wasn't going to branch out into hippotherapy, despite what they'd said when I was first hired. So what's the point? I don't want to be a regular OT. They do good work. It's just not for me." But what was for her? That was the big question that had no immediate answer looming on the horizon.

"You can't do the hippo whatever on your own?"

"Not without a master's. And even then, would you take Calvin to a solo practitioner for something like that? Wouldn't you want a bigger office of staff behind them? For that matter, I could handle doing the therapy, no problem, but the rest?" Sophie shook her head. "I don't think I could do that all on my own. Insurance claims. Governmental oversight. I don't even know what would be involved in that."

"There might be other people looking to transition to a different sort of practice." Maria filled the mugs with hot water and slid the box of tea bags over to Sophie before choosing one of her own and dunking it. "I'm just throwing out ideas. It seems to me, you owe it to yourself to do what you can to chase your dream. Or at least explore all the options before you write it off. Pray about it."

"Sure." Sophie frowned into the mug. Was there any point in praying about it? She didn't know the first thing about setting up her own therapy office. Did people even do that? And her degree

—she hadn't officially withdrawn. What would it take to finish? "What's new with you?"

Maria glanced over her shoulder before leaning closer and lowering her voice. "I'm pregnant. You can't tell anyone. I haven't even told Cyan yet. I'd planned to do something special this weekend, but now I'm not sure if he'll be back or if that's even going to be a good idea. I've been bursting to tell someone."

"Wow. Congratulations." Sophie took the tea bag out of her mug and set it on the wrapper. "That's big news!"

Maria nodded. "It's going to change a few things, but Betsy and Wayne were so good about flexibility the first time around, I think it'll be okay. Plus, Cyan works at home. So between the two of us, we should be able to juggle."

"Do you think Calvin will be excited?" Sophie had thought having a younger sister was going to be like having a doll to play with. She hadn't banked on a little usurper instead of a friend.

"I hope so. He seemed on board with the idea when we discussed the theory, but . . ." Maria shrugged. "You know how kids are. I'm not sure he really understands what it'll mean. No one does, until the baby's there."

Sophie chuckled. "True. It'll be different for Calvin than it was for me—he's old enough to help. And a baby won't really be competition."

"Except for time." Maria sipped her tea. "I'm worried about that, a little. Babies take up time, and Calvin's used to having both Cyan and me whenever he wants us."

"I think he'll be okay. He's a smart kid. And a good one. He'll understand." Sophie took a drink, scalding her tongue slightly. "I'll pray for that, at least."

"Thanks. I appreciate it." Maria checked the time and set her tea aside. "The guys should start showing up any minute now. Would you help me set up?"

"Sure." Sophie stood and came back around into the kitchen.

"Do you think I should touch base with Royal and just let him know I heard?"

"I think that's a lovely idea." Maria reached into a cabinet for a small stack of plates that she handed to Sophie. "Why don't you set these out and do that?"

Sophie took the dishes and set them in front of the seats at the counter, then grabbed her cell. She tapped out a quick text.

RAN INTO MARIA, SHE TOLD ME ABOUT YOUR DAD. SO SORRY. LET ME KNOW IF I CAN HELP.

She paused and frowned at the phone before tacking on: *PRAYING FOR YOU.*

Sophie hit send and put her phone back into her pocket. That was enough. She didn't need to pester him while he was dealing with family tragedy.

But she missed him.

Probably more than she should.

Royal shifted awkwardly in the chair. It wasn't *un*comfortable. But he wasn't going to be looking into ordering some for himself. The small room was obviously meant to be comforting and warm, but it still felt like the funeral home that it was.

His mom reached over and took his hand. "Thanks for coming with me."

"Of course. You know any of us would have come." Or all of them. Really, though, he wished Azure was here. She was going to try and zip out, but Mom was on a tear that everything had to be decided right now. "You remember there's not a big hurry."

"No. I want to get it done. Move on."

Move on? He cleared his throat. "I know the two of you were having trouble—"

"Don't. Okay? Please just don't." A tear rolled down her cheek, followed quickly by another. "I loved your father. I haven't liked him very well since April, but I loved him. Even though he apparently didn't feel the same toward me."

"Mom." Royal squeezed her hand. There weren't words. What was he even supposed to say? He knew his dad had loved his mom. Maybe he was terrible at showing it—well, obviously he was—and the whole situation with Jade was awful, but Royal refused to consider the possibility that his parents would have split up. Not after all these years. It was better not to dig into it. She could feel how she felt. "You're sure about cremation?"

"That's what he wanted. It always has been." She sighed and reached for the binder in the middle of the table. She flipped open the cover.

Royal glanced at the first page. There were so many different types of urns. "And the ashes? You'll keep them?"

"Oh, no. No. I'll bury them. Find a cemetery somewhere. He liked it here, in Arizona. There's probably one here where I could get him a spot."

"That'll be nice? You can visit if you want." Was that a thing? Did people visit interred ashes? Surely they did. Would his mom?

She shook her head. "I guess we'll see. I'm not sure I'll stay. I —your father handled the bills. The house. I have my own account for my business, but it's not enough to sustain me, I know that. I guess we'll have to see what there is."

"I can help you figure things out. Or Cyan." Cyan was a better choice.

"You can both come to the bank. I thought we'd do that tomorrow. I might need a death certificate. I guess that's something to ask. Could you write it down?"

Royal pulled out the little spiral notebook his mother had handed him before they left and flipped it open. The first page was already half full with questions and thoughts. Royal wrote down the question about the bank and jotted a few additional notes of his own.

"What do you think of this one?" Mom tapped a simple, marble box. It showed several color options, one of which was a deep blue.

"He'd like the blue."

"He would, wouldn't he? Or he would have." She swallowed and looked away. "It's hard to think of him in the past tense."

"Do you think . . . he grew up with Grandma and Grandpa. Church. God. I know he never really embraced it while we were kids, but is there any chance he believed underneath it all?"

"Oh, Royal. I don't know what to say. I don't believe there's something else, you know that. All we get is this life. You live it as best as you can, then you die and it's over. Heaven? Hell? You'll have to ask your grandparents." She tapped the picture again. "I think this one. In green."

"It's a good choice. You don't want to look through and make sure there's not something else that would be better?"

Mom's lips curved and she shook her head. "No. That's the difference between your father and me. I've always known what I wanted when I saw it. And I stopped looking. He could never shake the idea that something better—bigger and more wonderful—might be around the corner. Tell me about Jade."

Royal blinked. "Tell you what?"

"About Jade. Skye mentioned you had dinner with her when you were out this way. Should I feel bad that she never got to meet her father?"

Royal's phone buzzed in his pocket. He fished it out as much to see who was texting as to buy some time. Sophie. He winced. He'd meant to text. Or call. Calling would have been better. He'd slept most of the way to Arizona, and once they'd arrived, they'd been going non-stop. But still. He could have gotten in touch.

He read the text and smiled.

"Who's that?"

"Sophie. She's praying for us."

"That's nice." His mom opened her mouth to say more, but the door to the little room swung open, and a clean-cut man in a dark suit stepped in.

"I'm so sorry to keep you waiting, Mrs. Hewitt."

Mom smiled. "It's Elise, and it's no trouble. This is my son, Royal."

"It's good to meet you. I'm Jerome and I'll be coordinating for you on our end." He pulled out a chair and sat, nodding to the binder. "I see you've been looking through the book. Do you have any questions?"

"I don't think so. We liked this one. In the green." Mom tapped the page.

Jerome swiveled the book so he could see and nodded. He flipped to the back of the binder and removed a sheet of paper and began to write. "Will you have a service?"

"I hadn't—Royal?"

"Um." Royal chewed his lip. "It's really your call, Mom. Do you have friends who would want to come? Neighbors?"

She shook her head.

"Do you want to have something? Or, I mean, Grandma and Grandpa are here. We could do something less formal at the house. Just family." Royal glanced at Jerome. "How long will it be before we can bring him home?"

"Probably a week. Possibly a little longer."

Royal nodded. Was he supposed to stay here that long? Was everyone? That wasn't really what he'd planned at all.

"Of course, you don't need, necessarily, to have the remains at a service. Some prefer it. Others don't." Jerome folded his hands. "It's entirely up to you. We do have rooms here where you can meet, if you don't have a house of worship you wanted to use."

"No. Nothing like that." Mom blinked away tears and stared at the wall. "We can talk to everyone about doing something with the family. It'll take me some time, I imagine, to find a place to have him interred. That's the word, right?"

"Yes." Jerome scooted his chair back and selected another

binder from the shelves along one wall. "If you don't have a plot already, we work with all the local cemeteries. I have their brochures."

Mom reached for the glossy, folded papers that Jerome offered. "Thank you."

"All we really need to firm up is the urn, which we've done. And then we should go over the information that will go on the death certificate to ensure it's all spelled correctly. Once that's finalized, we'll get you copies, as you'll need them for settling the estate."

Royal's phone buzzed in his pocket. Was it Sophie again? Was it wrong that he'd rather be at the ranch with her than sitting here? No. Life was for living. He disagreed with his mom about heaven and hell, but she wasn't wrong about the fact that God put us on Earth for a reason. He believed, more each day, that Sophie was part of that reason for him.

"Do you need to get that, honey?"

"No. Sorry." Royal dragged his thoughts away from the ranch and Sophie and listened to his mom go over the data of his dad's life. How could she be content with that being it? All that was left? It was heartbreaking. He was going to do better about praying for Mom. She needed Jesus.

"If you'll give me a few minutes, we'll get this typed up and printed out. I'd like you to go over it one more time when it's done so that we're sure to get all the correct information on there." Jerome stood with the papers in his hand. "Can I offer you a beverage while you wait?"

"No. Thank you." Mom blinked, her eyes still glassy with tears.

Royal slipped his arm around his mom's shoulders and pulled her close. "I love you, Mom."

"Love you, too, baby. I'm sorry your last time with Dad was so hard."

"Yours, too." Royal rested his head against his mom's. Was there something else he should have done? Maybe. But there were always regrets of some sort. "I think Dad knew we loved him. I'm not sure what more we could have done."

She nodded. "And Sophie?"

"What about Sophie?"

"Does she know you love her?"

Love her? He shook his head. "Mom . . ."

"Oh, Royal. Don't be that way. It's easy enough to see if someone's looking. I was looking. Don't take too long to figure it out for yourself."

In love with Sophie?

He liked her.

They were friends.

He wanted to spend more time with her.

More time kissing her.

Did he love her?

How was he supposed to know?

"How are you? How's your mom?"

Royal stretched out on the couch in his parents' living room and held the phone up to get a better angle of his face on the screen. "She's resting. Cyan, Indigo, and Skye took the grandparents out to lunch. I volunteered to hang here in case Mom needs something. I don't think she's been out of her room all day."

"It's hard."

"Yeah. I wish you were here."

Sophie smiled. "Me, too. I could drive out if you needed?"

"No. It's seven hours. And I think we're heading back tomorrow anyway. Grandma and Grandpa are going to go down to Indigo's and load up the animals and bring them back. Indigo will help Mom get settled and then come to the ranch."

"Wow. She's really coming." Sophie frowned. "Can one animal trailer really fit all the livestock your sister has?"

"She says yes. I don't know if she's bringing them all. Or maybe she said, and I was distracted."

"No one could blame you. Are you okay?"

"I don't know." Royal sighed. "I hate knowing that the last time I saw my dad, he was storming off. And it wasn't my fault, but I still feel guilty. Should we have gone after him?"

"I don't know. Your mom said not to. I don't think you should second-guess."

"That's what Grandma said. It's hard."

Sophie nodded. "I'm sorry."

"Tell me something else. Something happy. How's the job search going?"

"Did you want something happy?"

Royal chuckled. "It can't be that bad."

"I'll send you my résumé. You can see that it absolutely can be that bad. I'm not qualified for anything other than flipping burgers. Or answering phones. At least phones would be a little less humiliating."

"There's nothing wrong with reception work. I've done that."

"Seriously?" Sophie squinted. "I'm trying to get a picture."

"Stop." He laughed. It was good to laugh—to let go for a minute of the heavy weight that pressed down on him otherwise. "I'm just saying, it's respectable work. So is burger flipping, for that matter."

"Yeah, I know. It's just not what I want to do."

"What do you want to do?" Royal watched the emotions play across her face.

"I was talking to Maria and she had an interesting thought. I'm not sure it could work—it seems impossible."

"But?"

She grinned. "But I'm praying about it. And doing some research."

"Well? Don't keep me in suspense."

"You know I was doing a master's to be qualified to do OT—hippotherapy, specifically?"

"Right. I thought you said there weren't other therapy offices in town."

"There aren't. But maybe there should be." Sophie bit her lower lip. "Maybe I could start my own practice—one that specializes in alternative therapies that my old office didn't do. Or only did grudgingly."

"Wow. You can do that?"

"I don't know. Like I said, I'm researching. And praying. And, I was wondering . . ."

Royal lifted his eyebrows.

"Would you maybe want to pray about it, too?"

He nodded. He wasn't the best at praying yet. It was all new to him. But maybe it wasn't something that had a skill level associated with it. He'd have to talk to his grandparents about that. Because while he wasn't convinced his mom was right about him being in love with Sophie, he definitely cared and wanted the best for her. "Yeah. Of course."

"Thanks. So, you think you'll be home tomorrow?"

"Or the next day. I'll keep you posted."

"Do that. I can't wait to see you."

Everything in him warmed even as he ached to be able to hold her. "Same goes."

16

E ven without a job, Mondays stank.

Sophie pushed away from her kitchen table and pressed her fingers to her eyes. A headache was brewing along with an impending sense of doom. She couldn't do this. She should admit it and start looking at realistic job options. Even if it meant moving.

Her parents had basically said exactly that at lunch after church yesterday.

She sighed. Was it positive or negative that their hilarity over the prospect of Sophie striking out on her own as an OT had taken the place of yet more wedding plans for her sister?

Sophie was going to call it neutral.

Her heart lifted as her phone rang. Maybe she could talk Royal into an afternoon ride. Except, she frowned at the number on the display, it wasn't Royal. "Hello?"

"May I speak with Sophie Ellison, please?"

"Speaking." She wandered to the fridge and pulled it open to stare at the contents.

"My name is Alicia Warren. I'm friends with your sister's fiancé's parents."

Well. That was a bizarre connection. Sophie shut the fridge and reached for a glass. Crossing to the sink, she turned on the tap. "Okay?"

"I was over there last night for dessert—my late husband and I used to play bridge with them. Now we mostly get together for pie. Anyway, Jamie mentioned that you were considering opening an occupational therapy office focused on hippotherapy."

Sophie took a sip of her water. "I'd been thinking about it. I made the mistake of mentioning it. Between my family and a solid week of research, I'm not sure it's the right direction. But I'll be sure to thank Jamie for mocking me behind my back next time I see him."

Alicia chuckled. "He wasn't, actually. He knows that my husband and I used to do it and thought I might be interested."

"You used to do equine therapy? Here? In town?" Sophie had never heard of anyone offering the service. Not in her lifetime, at least.

"No. Outside Santa Fe, and well before your time." There was a smile in the woman's voice. "But Jamie thought it might be a good idea for me to reach out and offer any advice I had."

"That was nice of him." Nicer than Sophie would have given him credit for. He never seemed to pay any attention to her—he was absorbed in Karla. Or so it seemed. Maybe she hadn't given him a fair shake. "But I just don't see it as being a practical thing now that I've started really looking at what's involved. I don't even have my degree yet—between that and the business loans and the insurance? Let alone the fact that I'm not convinced I'd have a big enough client load to make it worthwhile. I think I'm better off looking in another direction. But I appreciate the call."

"Those are certainly concerns. I take it you have lots of horse experience?"

This lady was not taking a hint. Sophie swallowed a sigh.

"Yes. I give lessons."

"Have you considered offering therapeutic lessons?"

"I'm not qualified yet."

"No, no. Not actual therapy—but I assume you've taken some of the classes, done research on what works and why."

"Sure, but—"

"Hear me out. The very act of being on a horse can be therapeutic. Adding in periods of trotting has been shown to calm children with ADHD. Others have benefitted from arm exercises while on horseback to help with additional core stabilization. These are things you could offer without calling it hippotherapy. It wouldn't be medical. Parents would simply be signing their children up for horseback riding lessons that had a little extra added on."

Sophie bit her lip. It was tempting. But it was also concerning. "Wouldn't I get in trouble?"

"No more than any other practitioner of alternative medicine."

"Aren't they all doctors, though?"

Alicia laughed. "Oh, my dear, no. Some are, certainly. But not all. And at the end of the day, you're not going to harm someone by teaching them to ride a horse."

"Well. That's not entirely true. People get injured all the time from falls or kicks—there are waivers."

"You're scrupulously honest, aren't you?" She paused. "I mean that as a good thing. Of course, it's possible someone could be injured. That's true regardless of what sort of riding lessons you're offering. It has nothing to do with any additional movement they're doing while on horseback."

Okay. That was true. "I'm not exactly swamped with students. I lost two because I was honest with their parents about the likelihood of them ever making the Olympics. I really only have one left, and she's occasional."

"That's actually where I might be able to help you. My granddaughter Lani is six, mad for horses, and also rather hyperactive. Her mother—my daughter-in-law—is determined that it's just age. But I've been around enough special-needs children to recognize what her mother won't see. I don't think I'd ever convince her to try occupational therapy. But horseback riding? That's something she's actively looking into. They've met with two stables in the area so far and are considering schedules."

Sophie set her basically untouched glass of water down and thought hard. It would still be a scramble to get students. She'd need to buff up her website, talk to the Hewitts about possibly spending more time with the horses. They were all easy tasks. "What would you need me to do?"

SOPHIE BATTLED the urge to jump up and down. Or possibly do a little dance, though dancing was definitely not one of her spiritual gifts. Instead, she waved goodbye to Lani, her mother, and Alicia as they loaded into Alicia's minivan. Lani had loved the trial lesson—and no one had balked at incorporating some seated exercises into the trips around the ring. Then, at the end, Sophie had nudged Blaze into a trot and they'd circled the ring for a solid five minutes. It might not be long enough to make a difference, but there were studies that suggested extended trotting could help with sensory regulation. And again, it didn't hurt anything. At worst? It was good exercise for Blaze.

Now, Sophie had to wait. Lani's mom had said she'd be in touch, but hadn't given any sort of indication *when*. Even still, Sophie was going to give this a shot and see what happened. If she could make enough to eke by giving lessons, she'd prefer that to rolling in cash doing something she hated.

Not that jobs where rolling in cash was an option were going to fall into her lap.

But the principle was there, nonetheless.

When the minivan started down the driveway, Sophie squealed and turned. She was bursting to tell Royal.

She ran to his cabin, gave a perfunctory knock, and pushed open the door. Before she could call out, she heard his voice coming down the hallway.

"You know it, sweetheart." He laughed and his voice was husky as he spoke. "Yeah, I miss you too. Anytime, babe. Bye."

Sophie's heart sank and she tried to back out of the door before he saw her. Had their kisses meant nothing? Of course, it was all a big joke to him. A woman in every port—that was the Royal Hewitt that existed online. And he didn't usually settle for just one.

For all Sophie knew, he had someone else in town on a string and that was why he'd been busy.

Stupid.

She was such an idiot.

Sophie turned and started to run as her eyes filled.

"Sophie?" Royal called out. Footsteps crunched gravel. "Hey! Wait up!"

Sophie jerked her arm away from his grasp and shook her head. "Leave me alone."

"What's wrong?" Royal darted in front of her, his arms nipping around her as she tried to zigzag away. "Hey."

Sophie refused to meet his gaze. She stared blindly over his shoulder. "I shouldn't have come in without knocking."

"What? No, it's fine. I don't have any secrets. I'll have to remember to lock the door when I shower though." He gave a low chuckle. "Not that I'd mind you walking in, but I'm not that guy anymore."

Sophie snorted. "Right."

"Whoa. Where'd that come from?"

Sophie wriggled out of his grasp and didn't even try to stop the venom that oozed into her voice. "Why don't you ask your *sweetheart*?"

Royal frowned. "I did. I asked you."

"Whatever." Sophie stepped back as he reached for her again. "Don't touch me."

He held up his hands and slowly put them in his pockets. "Can we talk? I don't know what I did—or what you think I did, because I can promise you I haven't done anything wrong."

Of course he hadn't. They hadn't had any conversations about exclusivity. They hadn't even been on another official date. But the road trip—the kissing—it meant something very specific to Sophie.

It clearly meant nothing to him.

Sophie swallowed. "I can't right now."

"Soph. Come on."

The concern on his face nearly had her caving, but she shook her head. "I need to go. I have stuff to do."

It wasn't a lie. There was a lot to do if she was going to push on the lessons. She had to take it seriously. Be professional.

She forced her lips into a smile. "I'll call you later."

"Sophie."

"Bye, Royal." She forced herself to walk rather than run to her truck. The dents on the hood that she still hadn't fixed broke her heart. She didn't have the money for the body work. It was all cosmetic—the mechanic who'd fixed the smashed engine assured her there wasn't an issue with leaving the body work for another day.

The truck might be damaged, but at least it was enough.

Even if Sophie never would be.

17

Royal watched her go, baffled. He wanted to chase her and demand that she explain what was going on, but he also didn't want to hurt her more than she was already hurting.

What was he supposed to do?

"Hey man, whatcha doing?" Tommy clapped Royal on the shoulder. "I think we're gonna tackle the big boss tonight. You want in?"

Video games. Royal nodded. At least that was predictable. "You know anything about women?"

Tommy snorted. "I have an ex-wife who barely lets me see my daughter. You tell me."

"That would be a no." Royal sighed and dragged a hand through his hair.

"Trouble with Sophie?"

"Apparently. But I have no idea what I did."

Tommy laughed. "That's never good. Apologize. When in doubt, apologize. Preferably with flowers."

"Shouldn't I know why I'm apologizing?"

"Ideally, yeah, but man, women aren't going to tell you what you did. You have to figure it out. Might as well just accept the blame, smile, and say you're sorry."

Royal studied the ranch hand. He didn't know Tommy as well as he did Morgan. They played video games together—with the whole group—but had only had a handful of conversations. "I'm not sure I have the right to ask this, but if you did that, why is your wife an ex?"

Tommy shook his head. "That's a question. I've asked her— I'm willing to do anything to be in my daughter's life. She won't explain. I guess sometimes things just don't work out. So I go up there every month to visit. Sometimes I get to take her to dinner. Sometimes I don't. It's always worth the effort."

"Why aren't you angry? Or fighting? If you got a lawyer—"

Tommy held up a hand. "Don't. It's not worth it. Anger would only hurt me. And I could never afford a lawyer who had a chance of beating what she'd come at me with. She has the backing of her real estate developer family. I'm just a ranch hand."

Royal bit back a comment. It wasn't his fight. If Tommy was okay with it, then that was all that mattered. "Do you know when my grandparents are getting back with Indigo's animals?"

"Tomorrow morning. They're stopping in Albuquerque for the night."

Royal lifted his eyebrows.

"They called Joaquin when we were finishing up the paddock fencing this afternoon. I guess they're worried about some of the roads in the dark with the length of the livestock trailer. Even with the hassle of feeding and watering overnight, they think it's safer to wait." Tommy shrugged. "Probably get here in time for lunch."

Royal nodded. Maybe this thing with Sophie could wait. He'd like to talk to his grandfather about it. Wayne and Betsy had been married a whole lot of years—that had to have given Wayne some insight about women that would help Royal navigate whatever was going on with Sophie. "What time tonight for the boss battle?"

"Seven? I think Morgan had some paperwork he needed to finish after supper. You wanna hang at my place?"

"Nah, man, I finally got my console hooked up. I want to give it a shot and see how the setup works."

"You get furniture yet?" Tommy laughed.

"Sort of." Royal shrugged. He'd found enough that would work—it wasn't exactly what he wanted, but there was nothing wrong with it. He'd convinced himself that the garage sale esthetic was fine for now, because when he and Sophie got married, she'd either have her own already or want to be part of the selection process.

Had he been completely off base?

She'd given him so much grief about his life before he came to Christ. Was that all talk? Was it possible she was one of those women who was happy to hop into bed with anyone who asked? Sophie hadn't shied away from their kisses—she'd been a full and active participant. But she also hadn't pushed for more when Royal had eased off.

Tommy gave him a strange look.

"Sorry. Mind's wandering. Shoot me an invite when it's time. I'll be ready."

Tommy tossed a sketchy salute and headed off toward his cabin.

Royal frowned.

He had a lot of experience with women, but very little understanding of how relationships worked. At least the kind of relationship he wanted now. In the past, whatever was going on with Sophie would've been a clear indication that their time together was over.

That wasn't what he wanted anymore.

He needed to fix this.

But how?

ROYAL SPOTTED Sophie in the riding ring and grinned. Finally. She'd been dodging him for a week and a half, but she couldn't get away now.

He forced himself to stroll casually in that direction. He'd been talking to his grandfather about Sophie since they got back. He'd even talked to Skye. And Cyan. Everyone agreed that communication was a vital part of a relationship. They'd also all encouraged him to pray about it.

He had been.

Royal wasn't sure if today's decision to corner her at the riding ring was a nudge from the Holy Spirit or the result of his own impatience. But it was super hard to communicate and clear the air when the person he most wanted to talk to wouldn't answer his calls or texts.

He propped a foot on the lower rail of the fence and leaned on the top. The current student wasn't one he recognized. The girl looked younger than Allie had been—six or seven, maybe? He wasn't great with kid ages, but she was definitely younger than Calvin.

He smiled. Calvin was a pistol. He'd taken to stopping by Royal's cabin on his way home after school every day and Royal was starting to look forward to the twenty or so minutes spent detailing the ins and outs of life as a third grader in public school. It was so different from Royal's own homeschooling experience on the bus they'd grown up in. A few weeks ago, the kid had even stood up to a bully. His parents weren't thrilled that he'd done it with his fists, but Royal could kind of see

Calvin's train of thought. Right or wrong, it had solved the problem.

It wasn't as though he hadn't known kids in public school but for whatever reason, hearing Calvin talk about his day was different.

Maybe Royal just loved being an uncle.

Sophie glanced over, and her expression froze. If she'd been a super hero, ice bolts would have shot out of her eyes and stabbed through his skull. It made no sense.

He smiled and lifted a hand in greeting.

She straightened her spine and spun back to her student.

Well, that was fine. He didn't need to interrupt her lesson. He could wait.

Sophie adjusted the little girl's heels in the stirrups and nodded. Then she held out her arms and waited until the girl followed suit. "Good. Now try to tighten your tummy and stay just like that while we walk."

What was she doing? This wasn't at all like the lessons she'd given Allie and her sister. The girl bobbled some and Sophie reached up to steady her. Then they stopped. Royal couldn't quite catch the words Sophie spoke—was she keeping her voice low on purpose? So he couldn't hear? No, that was being paranoid. He might not understand what happened to make her disappear, but he wasn't going to descend into paranoia just yet.

Sophie checked the girl's grip on the saddle, and then took the lead and started to jog. The horse eased into a trot. Royal smiled as the girl bumped up and down and grinned like she'd never done anything more fun. It wasn't his favorite activity, but he was glad someone enjoyed it.

They trotted the circumference of the ring for a long time. Each time they passed him, Royal waved at the little girl, and she hollered back hello.

Sophie ignored him. Pointedly.

When they finally stopped, Sophie helped the little girl dismount and led the way to the gate out of the ring.

A woman came jogging up. "I'm so sorry. Am I late? I got caught up."

"You're right on time. We had a good ride, right, Lani?"

"Mama! It was fun!" The girl bounced to her mom and took her hand. She stayed there, attached at the hand but still jumping, leaning, tugging, and spinning while her mother spoke to Sophie.

"See you next week, Lani. Thanks again."

"Thank you." The woman smiled. "Come on, Lani. Let's go home and eat lunch."

"Yay!" The girl bounded off toward the main parking area of the ranch in front of his grandparents' house.

Sophie led the horse out of the ring and started toward the stable.

"Wait up." Royal jogged until he could fall into step beside her. "Hi."

"What do you want, Royal?"

No small talk then. Okay. He rearranged his plan of attack. "I want to know why you disappeared. You're obviously upset with me. But I don't have any idea why."

"Seriously?" She stopped and frowned at him, one hand on her hip. "You disappear on me without a word. And okay, great, I get it—you had to rush off because of a family emergency, but you could've sent a text. I had to hear about it from Maria."

He winced. "I—"

She held up a hand. "Not finished. I got over that, mostly. I mean I can't promise letting you know would have been my first thought if something happened to my parents—not when we hadn't even taken the time to define whatever was between us."

Was between them? He opened his mouth again but closed it when she shook her head.

"So okay. That was on me, and I handled it. Until I walk in on you basically having phone sex with someone."

"Having—what? I don't even know what you're talking about? I've never had phone sex, to start with, and even if that was something I used to do, it wouldn't be something I do now. Especially not when I'm in a relationship with you!" Royal took a deep breath. Yelling wasn't going to solve anything, but he couldn't shake the idea that it might make him feel better. Where on earth had she gotten this? Did she lie awake at night thinking of ridiculous accusations to toss around?

"Whatever. I heard what I heard."

"But you didn't! When did this supposed conversation happen?" Royal crossed his arm.

"A week ago Monday. Right before I walked out and reminded myself why I don't date."

Last Monday? He'd had a couple of phone calls from authors he'd interviewed on his podcast when they had new releases and one of them was interested in him doing the audio for her new book. But that was . . . "Karen? You can't possibly mean Karen. She's like seventy."

Sophie shrugged.

A smile tugged at the corner of his lips. "Happily married more than fifty years, with like ten grandkids and her first great-grand on the way."

"So you like older, married women. It's not like fidelity is something you were raised on."

Royal leaned back and cocked his head to the side, his tone turning to ice. "Excuse me?"

"You heard me. I don't buy the fact that no one knew your dad was cheating on your mom."

"You don't have to buy it. None of the kids knew. Mom apparently did—she and Dad had some weird arrangement. One I think is pretty terrible, if you're wondering, and it's not some-thing I'd be a party to. You seriously think that little of me?"

Sophie jerked a shoulder and started walking again.

Royal watched her disappear into the stable as the future he'd been imagining with Sophie crumbled around him, leaving him numb.

Maybe there was nothing left to say after all.

18

S ophie fumed the whole time she groomed Blaze and cleaned the tack. Royal had a lot of nerve, acting like she was the one who'd done something wrong. Pfft. Whatever. If he thought he could prance around in his cabin talking on the phone in his husky bedroom voice and calling other women "sweetheart" while he was involved with her, he had another think coming.

Her high school boyfriend had been the same. He'd dated his way through the entire cheerleading squad and Sophie hadn't had a clue. She'd been the quiet, gullible, nerdy girlfriend helping him with homework, taking his dismissals of the snarky comments other girls made when she was around, and accepting that he had to run to practice. Even when practice hadn't started yet.

She'd just thought he was super dedicated.

To be fair, he was. Just not to her. Or to the sports he played. No, he was dedicated to making sure he got to as many bases as possible with as many girls as possible before he graduated.

Too bad there wasn't a *cum laude* for that. He would've gotten that cord for sure.

She blew out a breath and stalked to her truck. There was work to do on her website, and she was meeting another stable owner at two. She needed to find somewhere else to hold her lessons. Desperately.

"Sophie?"

Sophie kept walking. Maybe Betsy would think she hadn't heard her.

"Honey, wait, please."

Sophie's shoulders dropped and she stopped. She tried to smile as she turned. "Hello, Mrs. Hewitt."

"Oh, honey. It's Betsy. Even if you're angry at my grandson." Betsy's breath puffed as she closed the distance between them. She propped her hands on her hips and paused a moment to catch her breath. "I was hoping you'd stay for lunch."

Sophie shook her head. "It's not a good idea."

"What if it was just you and me?" Betsy smiled. "We could set up in the dining room, and you can tell me what's wrong."

"There's nothing wrong. Just a realization that we're incompatible." Because Sophie absolutely would not be with someone who wasn't one hundred percent committed to her. She wasn't open to any sort of arrangement. And even if Royal was telling the truth and the woman he'd been talking to wasn't interested in him—or interesting to him—romantically, she also couldn't be with someone who flirted like that. It might take her heart a while to catch up with her brain, but Sophie could wait it out.

"Because of Martin?"

"I don't—because he died? No."

Betsy chuckled and slipped her arm through Sophie's. "Come in the house and get a bite to eat. You can be stubborn and not talk, if that's what you want, but I think we've known each other long enough that I can be a little stubborn myself and insist you hear me out."

"Why?" Sophie sighed.

"We can start with the fact that I don't want to lose your business."

Sophie frowned. "I—what do you mean?"

"I mean that the Double P and the Bar Z both called to check and see what kind of stable tenant you were and if I would share whatever complaints I had about you since they were bad enough that I'd kicked you out." Betsy patted Sophie's arm. "They both know I'm a soft touch—and so is Wayne—so it had to be something pretty awful."

Sophie closed her eyes. She hadn't anticipated that. At all. She'd thought she was being so clever. "Mrs. Hewitt."

"Betsy."

"Betsy. I'm sorry. I just thought it'd be easier for everyone if I found someplace else. It's not fair for Royal to have to risk running into me all the time. He lives here."

"And is he upset with you?"

Until their conversation this morning, Sophie wouldn't have said so, but now? She nodded. "Most likely."

"Good." Betsy grinned and gestured for Sophie to go into the house.

"How is that good?"

"Because all this past week he's been moping and confused. Upset is progress."

She didn't want Royal to be any of those things. It was bad enough that her heart was breaking, Sophie didn't want to consider the possibility that he was in the same boat. "It's just more reason why I should go somewhere else. Of the two, do you have a recommendation? The other places around are all more expensive than I can manage right now. But those two are at least possibilities."

"Hmm. I guess if you're adamant, I'd try the Bar Z first. I've known Henry and Rita a lot of years and they're good people. Not that the folks at the Double P aren't. I just don't know them as well. That said, I'd still like a shot at convincing you to stay here."

"Mrs.—" She broke off at Betsy's raised eyebrow. "Betsy. I don't see it being possible. I can't concentrate on my lessons knowing Royal could show up at any time. And then, if he does show up, it takes all my concentration to ignore him. My students deserve better."

"That they do." Betsy gestured to the dining room. "Go take a seat. I'll be back in one second with the food."

"I don't—" Sophie frowned as Betsy disappeared down the hall to the kitchen. The woman wasn't kidding when she said she was going to be stubborn. But this was a meal she didn't have to make. Or pay for. So she should probably be grateful. Slowly but surely, Lani's mom was spreading the word about Sophie's lessons. She had two new students starting next week. But the trickle of income wasn't going to be enough in the long term. Realistically, she needed at least two students a day, five days a week if she was going to cover bills. And that didn't include sibling discounts, which she felt obligated to offer.

"Here we are." Betsy came back with two plates and two cans of soda. She set down the food, took a seat, and offered a short prayer. "Now. Let's talk a little about our current barn agreement."

❧

IT HAD BEEN like being smashed by a quiet, grandmotherly steamroller. Sophie still wasn't sure what had happened. One minute, she was eating her lunch and running through all the reasons why staying at Hope Ranch was the worst possible idea.

The next, she'd been taking on lessons as part of their camp offerings at a significant commission.

Nobody, it seemed, said no to Betsy Hewitt.

Sophie published the update to the main page of her website and logged out. She wandered to her little patio and stared out the window. It was the weird time of day when it wasn't dark, but it was after sunset. Everything was gray, but there weren't yet stars. It had been cold today. There was the possibility of snow next week. Would families really keep up their riding lessons through the winter like they said they would? It was easy to agree now, before being up on a horse was an exercise in not shivering off.

She'd just have to wait and see.

Betsy had dangled the carrot of an indoor ring. Why would the Hewitts do that? They made so little from her use of the horses and space. Why would they add an expense just to keep her around?

A knock at the door startled her.

She closed her eyes and leaned her forehead against the cold glass of the sliding door. Sophie couldn't deal with her mom right now. And there was no one else who would come by without calling first. Not even her sister—though that hadn't always been the case. Was it possible to rebuild that relationship without all the baggage of the past handful of years? After Jamie sent his parents' friend her way, Sophie felt like she owed it to Karla to try.

Another knock.

With a groan, Sophie turned from outside and stomped to the door. She wrenched it open. "Mom? I'm not—oh. It's you."

Royal held out an insulated cup from the local coffee shop in town. The faintest whiff of caramel hit her nose. "Can I come in?"

Sophie reached for the drink. Her voice was hard when she spoke. "Why? Didn't we say everything this morning?"

She was already close to tears—another run-in with Royal was bound to bring them. And that wasn't something she was willing to do in his presence.

"I don't think we did, actually." Royal lifted his eyebrows. "What do you say?"

She sighed and stepped back. "Fine. Whatever."

"Thanks." Royal grinned and stepped into her apartment, closing the door behind him. He looked around, nodding occasionally. "I like your place. It suits you."

What did that mean? It was small and a mishmash of things that had caught her eye. There was no overarching theme to her décor. It wasn't polished, like his grandmother's house. She shrugged and sipped her coffee.

"It's decaf. I thought, given the time, that was better." Royal wandered into the living space and settled in the rustic wooden rocker she'd talked her dad into letting her take when she moved out. "I was thinking about what you said this morning."

"Can we just not talk it to death? We want different things. It's better to figure that out now, isn't it?" Sophie sat on the couch and tucked her legs under her.

"That's the thing, though. I don't think we do."

She frowned.

"Karen Gillespie. That's the name of the woman I was talking to. I'll even own up to flirting, although I would say it was harmless."

Sophie snorted. Flirting was never harmless. There was—or there always should be—intent behind it. "You called her sweetheart."

"Well, she is one." Royal shrugged and took a sip. "I'm sorry it bothered you. I can't promise I'll never call someone else by an endearment, but I can promise to try not to."

"That's not the point."

"Isn't it? You still think, underneath it all, that I'm the guy who you see on the old episodes of my podcast and in my videos. You don't trust the new stuff—even though that's the guy you know in person."

"There's a lot more of the old guy to see." Sophie didn't like the sinking queasiness twisting in her gut. "Change takes time to be permanent."

"Yeah, okay. How long? How long will it be until you trust me?"

"I don't—that's not what's going on here." She wasn't the one at fault. He was! "You were the one flirting on the phone! Because I'm not enough for anyone. Not my parents. Not my sister. Not my students."

Royal leaned forward and set his coffee down on the table, concern written on his features. "Sophie."

She shook her head and looked away. Why had she said all that? She should have left it alone. Tears burned her eyes, and she bit her lip to keep them from falling. She wasn't adding that humiliation on top of everything else. "I think you should go."

Royal's hand gripped her shoulder. "I don't know how to prove to you that you are enough—for me and probably also for everyone else you named. And if they don't agree, that's their problem. But, Soph? You need to realize you're enough for you before any of that is going to matter. Or—maybe even more importantly—you're enough for God. He made you this way on purpose."

Sophie snorted. She knew that. Everyone was always telling her that. No one wanted to listen when she pointed out that it must have been a mistake. Or she'd messed it up somehow—it wasn't like God forced people to do exactly what He wanted.

Royal's lips brushed the top of her head. "And God doesn't make mistakes. Even though we might not understand all the ins and outs. I'll go, because you asked me to—but if it was up to me, I'd stay. I want to stay. I want to be with you. If you decide you'd like that, too, you know where I am."

She squeezed her eyes shut and covered her face with her hands. Royal's footsteps were light as he crossed to the door and let himself out. Swallowing the lump in her throat, Sophie gave in to the sobs that clawed at her soul.

19

Royal stood on the little makeshift patio in front of his cabin and watched Sophie stride toward the parking area in front of his grandparents' house. The effort she expended to not look in his direction was obvious—to him at least—in the set of her shoulders and the stiffness of her spine.

He sighed.

After their conversation on Wednesday, he'd hoped she might seek him out. She was at least responding to texts with single letters—a single word if she had to. But she didn't pick up if he called. She just texted back the word "busy."

"It's only been two days." Royal muttered to himself as he stepped onto the gravel path. Just because it felt like a lifetime didn't mean it had been one.

He wandered toward the stable, but rather than going in and seeking out Morgan, he kept walking. The bleat of sheep caught his attention, and he aimed in the direction of the new paddocks instead.

Joaquin stood in the middle of the alpaca space with an enormous rake. He was shaking his head and frowning.

"Hey, man." Royal lifted a hand as he approached the fence. "How's it going?"

"They poop a lot." Dragging the rake along behind him, Joaquin came over to the fence. "Seriously, between making sure they're fed and policing the poop, it's a lot of work."

"You didn't think it would be?"

"No. No, I did. I just also thought your sister would be here to help." He grinned and leaned on the top rail of the fence. "Have you heard anything from her about when she'll be heading this way?"

"Nope. I guess straightening everything out for Mom is taking longer than expected. The house—it's a mess."

"What do you mean?"

"I guess Dad didn't put Mom on the deed, and since they weren't legally married it's a bit of a nightmare. He didn't have a will, so all his assets are supposed to be divided among his heirs. And I guess that leaves Mom out. Or that's what her lawyer is saying."

"Ouch."

"Yeah." Royal pinched the bridge of his nose. There was also some concern that Jade was legally entitled to a share, and that wasn't going over with Mom at all. As far as he was concerned, it was the better thing—the right thing—to divide everything evenly between the six kids from the get-go. He would happily give his portion back to Mom, and he suspected most of the other kids would, too. Especially since his mom didn't really have any other means of support. "Mom makes lotion and soap and that sort of thing when she feels like it—she has a little online shop. But it's not really enough income right now. Maybe she can ramp things up. I don't know."

Joaquin nodded. "I guess it makes sense, then, for Indigo to stay out there a while. It's good someone can."

"Yeah. It's a relief, for sure. Although, if she couldn't, I'm sure

I could have gone out just as easily." Maybe he should offer anyway. See if Indigo needed a second set of hands.

"I thought you had work to do? Wasn't that the point of your little road trip?"

"Yeah. And I do. I've started recording the audio for an author and I have a couple of auditions out for others. It's a good new sideline." Royal shrugged. "But family's more important, and I'd set it aside if I needed to."

Joaquin laughed. "You're a Hewitt to the bone."

If he'd only had his dad's example to go by, Royal would never have agreed. Or he would've considered it a slam. After meeting his grandparents? "Thanks."

"I should get back to it. There are still some things over at the camp I promised your sister I'd get to today. If you talk to Indigo, let her know the herds are doing fine, would you?"

"Sure." Royal thought a moment. "You know, you could call her."

"What?"

"Indigo. It's okay if you call her yourself." Royal pushed off the fence and met Joaquin's gaze head on. "She'd probably appreciate it."

"I don't want to bother her."

"I know my sister well enough to say she'll let you know if you're a bother. Give her a call."

Joaquin frowned. "You won't tell her for me?"

"No, man, I will. I just think you should call her, too."

Joaquin's shoulder jerked. "I'll think about it."

"Good enough. Thanks for looking after her animals. I know she considers them family."

Another shoulder jerk, then Joaquin turned and trudged back to the pile of alpaca poop he was raking.

Royal smiled to himself. If he wasn't reading things wrong—and given his current situation with his own life, there was a reasonable probability that he was—Joaquin had a little thing for his sister. Or at least for her animals.

Had they met?

Royal searched his memory and came up blank. They'd talked on the phone, for sure. And some video calls. Maybe they hadn't met in person. It'd be interesting to see what happened when she moved out here after getting Mom settled.

"What are you smirking about?" Skye fell into step beside him.

"Where'd you come from?"

"I was at the stable, talking to Morgan. Now I'm heading back to the lodge. You?"

"I was heading to see you." He might not have originally had that destination in mind, but after seeing Joaquin and the animals, it was as good a next stop as any.

"Cool. You can help me move some furniture. Morgan can't get away until after supper." She bumped his shoulder. "So what caused the grin? You fix things with Sophie?"

Royal snorted. "No. I tried. Pretty sure I made it worse."

Skye's eyebrows rose. "How'd you do that?"

"She's convinced herself that she doesn't deserve me. Or happiness. Or anything, really." He shook his head. "I can't help her with that. Especially when she doesn't believe me when I say something."

"That's hard. Self-esteem is hard."

Royal glanced over at his twin sister. She'd know. She'd had her battles with self-esteem. Maybe she still did, but they weren't as bad these days. At least not that he'd noticed. "Any tips?"

"Not really. She has to decide that her value comes from Jesus. Until she's willing to accept that God made her the way she is for a reason—whether she thinks that reason is good, bad, or indifferent—she's never going to find someone or something else that makes her okay with herself long term."

Royal nodded. "That's basically what I told her. Wayne said something much like that when I first accepted Jesus. My whole life had been constructed in such a way—the influencing, the fame-seeking, all of that—it was hard to reconcile who Jesus said a believer should be and who the world expected me to be. I've lost sponsors. I've lost followers. I used to chase those like they were breath in my lungs. It was a constant worry that I didn't have enough, that I wasn't enough. Before, if I lost a follower, I'd obsess about it until I got at least five new followers. Lose a sponsor?" He shook his head. "You saw me this spring. I'm learning, slowly, to find my worth in Jesus now. But I get that it's hard."

Skye stopped and wrapped her arms around him. "Hard, but worth it?"

"Yeah." He stepped back. "Doesn't mean I have any idea how to help Sophie get there."

"You can't. I'm sorry." Skye opened the front door of the lodge. "But you can help me rearrange the fellowship room."

Royal chuckled. Maybe moving couches and tables would keep him from obsessing about Sophie. His mom was clever—whispering the idea that he was in love with Sophie into his subconscious. Now he couldn't get the thought out of his head.

He was in love with Sophie.

And she wanted nothing to do with him.

ROYAL SCANNED the rows of the church worship center. He smiled when he spotted Sophie. Glancing at his sister, he nudged her. "I'm going to see if I can sit with Sophie."

"She's here?" Skye grinned. "Good plan. We'll catch up after the service. I'll be praying for you."

"Thanks." Royal swallowed as his nerves jangled. Was it a

bad idea? Even if it was, he didn't care. He missed her. He slowed and slipped into the row where Sophie sat, scrolling on her phone. "Hey. Is this seat taken?"

Sophie looked up and her lips thinned. "No."

"Can I sit with you?"

"I guess."

It wasn't a rousing invitation, but he'd take it. "Thanks. How are you?"

Sophie shrugged and returned to her phone.

Okay. Well, he'd skip the small talk. At least she hadn't told him to go away. In his pocket, his phone vibrated. He slipped it out and glanced at the screen. Skye had sent him a string of emojis—thumbs-up, party horns, clapping hands. He laughed.

Sophie looked over. "What's funny?"

Royal angled his screen so she could see. "Skye's glad we're sitting together."

Sophie snorted, but the corners of her lips twitched.

"I am, too."

"Royal, I—"

Of course the worship leader chose that moment to strum his guitar and invite everyone to stand and worship Jesus.

"Could we grab lunch after church?" He held his breath.

Finally, she nodded. "Yeah, okay."

Royal smiled and faced the front, focusing on the words displayed on the screen before he joined in singing. His voice wasn't the best—or at least, that was what the voice in his head whispered to him—so he sang quietly. But for the first time in several weeks, he actually felt like singing. He was going to call it progress.

When the pastor asked them to open their Bibles to read along with him in Zephaniah, Royal frowned. That wasn't one he knew. He scrolled through the book listing in his Bible app and tapped it. Old Testament—that explained it. He'd been focusing on the New. Wasn't the Old Testament, well, old? There had certainly been plenty of sermons focusing on the fact that Jesus removed the need for all the rules and, at least to his mind, crazy, things God had required of Israel. History could be interesting, though, so maybe this was like a story?

"We'll be in chapter three starting at verse fourteen." The pastor waited as the rustle of Bible pages settled.

Royal followed along—smiling at the word picture of God dancing over him, singing and taking delight in him. He glanced over at Sophie.

Her brow furrowed as she stared at her phone.

Royal prayed that God would form the same picture in Sophie's mind that had formed in his. A picture of a loving God delighted in His child—not because of what the child had done, but because the child was worthy simply for being.

At the end of the sermon, Royal stood with the rest of the congregation to sing. Sophie stayed in her seat, her eyes closed.

When the service finished, Royal sat down again and waited. He wanted to reach out and take Sophie's hand. Or put his arm around her. Some sort of physical contact to let her know he was there and he cared.

But something in his spirit stopped him. Instead, he tapped a quick reply to Skye's text that he and Sophie were having lunch, and he'd get back to the ranch on his own. He hoped those plans were still in place. But if Sophie needed to go home, to have time to herself, he could always call an Uber.

The worship center was almost empty when Sophie looked up. She turned to Royal and bit her lip. "You didn't have to wait."

"I'd still like to grab lunch with you. If you want?" He was giving her an out. He hoped she wouldn't take it, but it seemed like the right thing to do. "I'll understand if you'd rather not."

"No." Sophie reached down for her purse before standing. "I'd like that, I think."

Royal stood too and held out his hand.

Sophie kept her gaze steady on his for the space of three heartbeats. Then she slipped her hand in his. "Am I driving?"

"Do you mind? I rode down with Skye and Morgan."

"I don't mind."

Things were still awkward between them, and he wasn't sure what would fix that. He stood by the fact that he hadn't done anything wrong. Sophie had jumped to conclusions based on the guy he'd been before he knew Jesus. And she hadn't been willing to trust him. That still stung. He followed her down the aisle, out into the parking lot, and to her truck.

"Feel like the cantina?" Sophie glanced over at him.

"Always." He squeezed her hand before dropping it to walk to the passenger side of the truck. He opened the door and climbed in. "Their enchiladas have ruined me for life."

She nodded and shifted into Reverse. "Hopefully we're not too late. There might be a wait."

"I don't mind if you don't. I've decided I'm going to try not to work on Sundays. I'm on schedule, so it's an easy decision—not sure if I'll make exceptions if I fall behind." Royal shrugged and looked out the window as they made their way through town. "But for now, a day with no business expectations sounds like a good thing."

"Schedule? What are you doing that has a schedule?"

Wow. He hadn't realized that Sophie missed all this—but of course she had. She'd cut him off because he'd been firming up the contract with Karen. "I'm recording an audiobook. It's more work, in some ways, than I realized it would be, but it's fun. It helps that the book is interesting."

"I didn't realize you'd signed a contract." She looked over and smiled. "Congrats. The equipment's working then?"

"It's great. I play back each chapter when I finish it—there's editing that has to happen—but the quality sounds good.

Karen's been pleased with the chapters I've sent her so far. It's a little like acting, to be honest. Actually . . ."

"Yeah?" Sophie braked and backed up before pulling into a parking spot that was a short walk from the restaurant but about as close as they were going to get if the traffic on the plaza was any indication. She shifted into Park and cut the engine before turning to look at him.

Royal turned to look at her. "There's a request out that I'd like to audition for—or at least it seemed like it'd be a good fit— but they want two voices. A guy to read the male voices and a woman to do the females. When I first saw it, I wanted to talk to you about it."

"Talk to me about narrating? I don't know how to do that." Sophie shook her head as she pushed open the truck's door. "That's insane."

"Or it's genius." Royal grinned as he hopped out of the truck and fell into step beside her. "One, it's extra money for you while you're building up your riding students. And if you liked it, we could make it a thing. Two, it'd be a chance for us to spend more time together doing something we enjoy."

"I don't know if I'd enjoy it. You're skipping that part. I'm not an actress."

"I don't consider myself an actor. It's different—look, would you be willing to give it a try? We could just play with it a little and see. If you hate it, no big, I'll let it go." Royal slid his hands into his pockets and tried not to look too hopeful. "Please?"

Sophie stopped and frowned. "Yeah, okay. We can play with it. But don't get your hopes up."

It was way too late for that, but Royal nodded.

There were already several groups holding pagers clustered together outside the cantina's bright teal door.

"Aw, man."

"Yeah. Maybe it's not too long." Royal touched Sophie's arm.

"Let me go in and see how long. I've got a hankering for those enchiladas."

She chuckled. "Okay. No more than hour. I mean it."

"Got it." He didn't want to even wait that long—he would, because the food here was amazing—but he'd be grumpy about it. He pushed through the clumps of people waiting inside and made his way to the podium. "How long is it for two?"

"Thirty to forty minutes."

"Okay. Can you put us down—table for two. Royal."

The harried-looking hostess scribbled on the clipboard, checked the number on the pager, and wrote it down before handing it to him.

"How far do these reach?" Royal held up the pager.

"There are some benches across the street by the adobe wall, if you don't want to wait by the door."

"Thanks." Royal tucked the pager into his coat pocket and headed back outside. He scanned the crowd for Sophie and found that she'd already made her way to the benches the hostess had mentioned. He jogged across and joined her.

"What'd they say?"

"Thirty-ish. I put us down." Royal pulled the pager out of his pocket and offered it to her.

Sophie waved it away. "You can hold it. Thirty minutes?"

"About. Maybe a few more. Why?"

"Because, Royal, we need to talk."

Her ominous tone made his stomach clench. She wasn't wrong—he'd just been hoping maybe they could find their footing a little better first.

20

Sophie stared straight ahead, not willing—or able, just yet —to focus on Royal.

We need to talk.

"Nothing good ever comes after that phrase. You know that, right?" Royal shifted so their knees touched. "Are you breaking up with me?"

She frowned, her head jerking to look at him. "You already dumped me."

"What? No, I didn't."

"Sure you did. You walked out of my apartment without looking back."

"After telling you I wanted to be with you, but that it was your choice." Royal shook his head. "How could you possibly have gotten that I wanted to break up out of that?"

Sophie hunched her shoulders. "You left."

"You told me to!" Royal scrubbed his hands over his face. "Was I supposed to stay? Then I would've been a bully for pushing you when you didn't want me around. I was trying to be polite."

She had seen it more as an unwillingness to fight for her.

One more example of her not being enough, not mattering enough to anyone. "Oh."

The conversation paused. Cold stung her cheeks, even though the sun was high in the cloudless, turquoise sky. No chance of snow today, that was for sure. How had she gotten everything so wrong? More to the point, had she been doing that her whole life?

"I'm sorry I made you feel that way. If I'd had any idea you were going to take it that way when I left, I would have stayed. I'm just sorry, in general. I never meant to hurt you. I'm sorry that I did."

Sophie reached for his hand. "I'm a big mess. Are you sure you want to be part of that?"

"More than anything." Royal laced his fingers through hers. "We're all messes, Soph. Some of us just hide it better."

She chuckled and her heart lifted. "I'm sorry, too. For all of it. I'm trying. I want to keep trying to be better. I'll probably get it wrong more than I get it right though, fair warning."

"Join the club." He bumped her shoulder. "I love you. We'll make it work."

Sophie's breath caught in her lungs. "What?"

Royal held her gaze. "I love you. You didn't know?"

She shook her head. "No one's ever said that to me before. I mean, my family, sure, but not someone who didn't have to."

"Well, I don't have to. I want to. But I will say, and I admit I've only spent time with your family the one time, that I don't think they only love you because they have to."

Maybe he was right. There were still a lot of things they said and did that made it feel like they considered her less than. Was it only because she allowed it to hurt her? "Maybe. Like I said, I'm working on it."

The buzzer in Royal's hand lit up and vibrated. "That was fast."

She nodded and stood. Maybe that was for the best. He loved her. And she wasn't sure how to respond. She liked him. A lot. They had chemistry, no question. But love? How was she supposed to know?

They had a quiet, comfortable meal. Conversation shifted between topics with ease. Royal never brought up love again, and Sophie wasn't going to be the one who did, either. Not that she had any idea what she'd say if it did get brought up. They'd known each other—sort of—since April. But how long had they been friends, really? Not much longer than the two months they'd been dating. Maybe things in TV shows or movies moved fast like that, but was it supposed to in real life?

Sophie snickered.

"What? I could use a joke."

She shook her head. "It's nothing."

They were walking out of the restaurant, back into the sunny cold. "Want to walk around the plaza for a little before we head back to the ranch?"

"Yeah, I'd like that. Maybe we could pop into one of the galleries that carry your sister's art? I haven't actually seen it." It was a good change of subject. Sophie wasn't ready to dive into relationship timing with Royal right now. She hadn't met Azure, but it seemed like everyone who found out Sophie worked at Hope Ranch commented on the woman's art. "It's supposed to be pretty special."

Royal grinned. "I'm biased, but yeah, it is. You'll see."

"What's it like to have family like that?" She should have stopped the words. If she'd realized they were coming out aloud, she would have. "Never mind. I shouldn't have—"

"Stop. You don't have to censor yourself. What are you getting at?"

Sophie sighed. "I'm jealous of your family, I guess. You seem so close to your siblings—all of them, not just your twin. Everyone loves each other all the time."

Royal laughed so hard he had to stop walking and bend over. "What?"

He shook his head. "No. It's not like that at all. I mean maybe, now that we're adults, it's easier. But we're also not living in each other's pockets anymore. I'm honestly curious to see how long before three of us being at Hope Ranch results in an epic sibling knockdown."

Epic sibling knockdown? "Nuh-uh. I can't see that at all. Especially not between you and Skye. You're twins!"

"What? You think twins don't fight? Please." Royal snorted. "I think the two of us were the worst growing up. Now that she has Morgan, it's easier. Now that we all have our own lives, it's easier. But we're family. We're going to fight. The difference is that we know, underneath it all, we have each other's backs. Always."

Sophie nodded. She felt that way about her sister. Even if it didn't seem like Karla felt the same. Although . . . had Jamie mentioned the riding thing to his parents on his own? Or was it possible that Karla had given him a nudge? Huh. That was something to consider. The more she thought about it, the more reasonable it seemed. "I guess maybe I have that, too. I just hadn't realized it. Thanks."

"Anytime." Royal squeezed her hand and stopped in front of what was considered the most prestigious gallery on the plaza. "In here."

"Here? I knew she was good. But in here? Really?"

"Really."

"Wow." Sophie reached for the door and smiled when Royal's arm snaked around her to grab it. He held the door as she went in. "Thanks."

"I think she's on the left, toward the back. Last I remembered, they had three of hers up, but I haven't been in in a while."

The gallery was packed with art that caught her eye. Bronze sculptures of horses bucking off rodeo cowboys. Turquoise and silver jewelry in settings that ranged from traditional Navajo to abstract modern interpretations. There was leather work and clothing. And paintings in every style imaginable.

At the back, Royal stopped in front of a large canvas that showed the *Sangre de Cristo* Mountains glowing in their signature red as the sun set. Everything in Sophie stilled.

What must it be like to have a talent like that?

She glanced at Royal and linked her hand with his. "It's beautiful."

Royal met her gaze and leaned his forehead against hers. "Not as beautiful as you."

"Stop." Sophie's cheeks burned, and she looked away. She wasn't under any illusion that she was gorgeous. She was passable—cute maybe. And yet, the idea that to Royal she exceeded that definition? It made her feel settled and warm. "Thanks."

"I mean it."

"I know you do." She might not understand it. But maybe she didn't have to. "You really want to try the two-person recording thing?"

If Royal was startled by the non sequitur, he didn't show it. Instead he grinned and nodded. "I really do."

Sophie took another long look at Azure's art before nodding. "All right, let's go give it a shot."

"Can you help me set up hay rides?" Skye jogged along beside Sophie as she led Blaze back to the stable after a lesson.

"Hay rides? Like in a wagon?"

Skye nodded. "At church yesterday, I got cornered by the children's minister. She wants to provide an alternative to Halloween."

"That's next week."

"Ten days. It's in ten days." Skye blew out a breath. "But I really think we can pull something together. And it'd be a great thing to offer—maybe something we can work in annually, like the sleigh rides at Christmas."

It wasn't a bad idea. It was just short notice. "What are you thinking? Full-fledged fall festival type thing? Or just a wagon full of hay pulled by horses?"

"I don't know? What do you mean fall festival?"

Sophie wrapped Blaze's lead around a hook and started removing her saddle. "I don't know. Bobbing for apples? A maze of some sort? Maybe face painting for people who don't already have a costume? A cakewalk?"

"I don't know if we could organize all of that in time. It sounds like a lot."

Sophie set the tack aside and reached for a brush. "It is. But what if we shot out a quick email to the various ministries and offered them a chance to set up a booth. If we sold tickets at the door, then we could split proceeds based on the number of tickets and it'd be a little fundraiser for them. They might not make much, but they could probably offset any costs at least. And knowing most of the folks who run things at church, they'll get the prizes and labor donated, so there won't really be costs to speak of."

"That's a great idea." Skye beamed at her. "You'll help me, right? Be the co-chair for this?"

Co-chair? That seemed like a lofty title for having an idea. But it wasn't like she had a lot else that needed doing. She had her students. And she and Royal were going to start on an audition for a Christian romance author who wanted dual narration.

But other than that, her schedule was wide open. "Sure. Why not?"

"Really?" Skye pulled Sophie into a quick hug. "When do you have time?"

"Now? I told your brother I'd come by for this audio project we're going to try after lunch. I'd planned to go home in between, but there's no reason I have to."

"Great. How can I help you finish up here?"

"If you want to wipe down the saddle," Sophie nodded to the cloth she used for that, "it's one less thing to do."

They finished quickly. Sophie gave Blaze a slice of apple she'd saved as a thank you for after lessons. Some of the other horses whickered in their stalls and she winced. "I didn't bring enough for everyone."

Skye laughed. "Morgan says they're all spoiled. They'll be okay. From what I gathered, Calvin's up here almost every day after school now begging to help. Usually his version of helping is giving them treats."

"Then I guess I won't feel too bad." Sophie dusted off her hands. "Where do you want to work?"

"Morgan said I could use his place—it's closer than going all the way back to the camp. I brought my laptop."

"He won't mind if I'm there?"

"Please." Skye grabbed her arm and tugged. "He considers you a friend."

He did? They had a cordial working relationship, but Sophie wouldn't have gone so far as to say they were friends.

"I do, too, for that matter. Probably everyone at the ranch does." Skye frowned as she glanced at Sophie. "Why do you look surprised?"

She hunched her shoulders. "I guess because I am?"

"Why?"

"Because I'm neurotic? I know—I'm working on it."

"So, you and my brother are . . .?"

"Friends?"

"Uh-huh. And?"

Sophie bit her lip. How much was okay to share? Would Royal be annoyed if she talked to his sister about things? Given her lack of other options, she'd risk it. "He said he loves me."

Skye squealed. "Really? That's so great! The two of you are so cute together."

"Are we?"

Skye sighed and put her hands on her hips. "Girl, I swear. Do you not take anything at face value? Ever?"

"I guess not. I'm used to looking for hidden barbs."

"They're usually there if you look hard enough. They just aren't always intentional. You should stop. Just accept that the words people say are the ones they mean."

"It's hard."

"Sure. But in the long run, it's easier. And maybe you'll miss some hidden digs, or someone will figure you're dense because you didn't call them out, but so what? You'll be happier."

It wasn't bad advice. Sophie wasn't sure it was good advice, though. Shouldn't she make sure she understood the intent behind what people said? "I guess I could ask for clarification if I'm not sure."

"If you have to." Skye shrugged and opened the door to Morgan's cabin. "Come on in. Want a soda? I stocked some diet in his fridge."

"Okay." Diet wasn't her favorite, but she could go with it. She glanced around the cabin—she hadn't been in Morgan's space before. "It's warmer than I thought it would be."

"Right? He actually decorated a little. Mind you, I have plans for when we're living at the lodge, but we can definitely use most of what he has here, too."

"How's that going—living over at the lodge?"

"I love it there. And it really is nice to be available when there are groups in. I have four writers there this week. Mostly they're keeping to themselves, but every now and then, one will have a question or need something. It's interesting, too." Skye pulled out a chair at the kitchen table and sat. "So Royal loves you. Do you love him?"

"That came out of nowhere."

"Come on, you know I had to ask. He's my brother."

Sophie sat and opened her soda. "I don't know how to answer."

Skye nodded. "It's tough."

"Yeah." Sophie took a long drink. "Can we do fall festival stuff?"

"Of course. Sorry. I don't mean to pry."

"You aren't. It's okay. I just don't know what to do about it. I like him. I like him a lot. More than I've ever liked anyone. And when he kisses me . . .sorry. That's probably TMI." Her face was hot. She twisted her fingers in her lap.

"No. I think it's good. I like knowing he's a good kisser. I suspect he's had a lot of practice. You don't mind?"

"Nah. He's not who he was." The words had the ring of truth. She'd known it. He'd said it. This time, she believed it. "He's a good man."

"He really is. Did you know he's pushing us—meaning the siblings—to give Jade an equal split of Dad's estate?"

"He is?" Sophie looked at Skye. "How do you feel about that?"

She shrugged. "I think I'm the only one who doesn't immediately have an issue with it. I don't like how she treated you when you had dinner with her. I really don't. But I also sort of understand it. At the end of the day, the way the law works, he died without a will. He and Mom weren't married—and I know it seems like common-law marriage is a thing, but there are only like eight states where it can happen, and even then it's not something that just occurs. People have to work to establish it. We never lived in any of those places anyway, so it's moot. According to the lawyer, his estate goes to his heirs. That includes Jade. Whether we like it or not."

"It's nicer, certainly, to just do it. You could make her sue you."

Skye chuckled. "And she'd sue for sure, don't you think?"

"I mean, given the one interaction I had with her? Yeah. I really think she would."

Skye nodded. "That's what I said. And it's only money."

Only money. It wasn't like the Hewitts—any of them—were rich. They had all their needs provided for, but none of them seemed to have a lot left over at the end of the day. Maybe Cyan, but only because he did some sort of fancy computer security work, so it seemed more likely. It wasn't as though he flaunted it. "Yeah."

Skye flipped open her laptop. "Fall festival."

"Right. Fall festival." Sophie paused, thought twice about her words, then spoke anyway. "Real quick—if I was in love with your brother, how would you suggest I let him know?"

21

R oyal made his way to the riding ring, barely able to control the grin that wanted to plaster itself across his face. He propped a foot on the lower rail and leaned on the top while he waited for Sophie to finish her lesson. She was up to a student every day—he knew that wasn't the load she needed, but it was a start. And word was spreading. But if she was worried about her bills, it was nice that he had good news tucked into his pocket that might just help.

"All right, let's trot." Sophie's voice was overly cheerful and Royal bit back a laugh as the kid on the horse groaned. "Aw, it's not that bad. And when we're finished, you can feed Cinnamon an apple slice. Deal?"

"Deal." The kid—he looked to be eight or nine—got a grip on the pommel of the saddle and nodded to Sophie.

Sophie urged the horse into a trot and she jogged alongside for the first lap of the ring. Then she slowed and let the horse keep going, calling out occasional encouragement.

Royal checked the time on his phone.

"They're trotting."

He glanced over at the woman who settled herself next to him at the rail. "Yes, ma'am. You're his mom?"

"Yep. He's mine. I wouldn't have believed that this would help if anyone other than Alicia Warren had suggested it." The woman shook her head. "I brought him last week for a trial lesson and they trotted for five minutes. We didn't have any meltdowns for a day and a half. Sophie says they're going to work up to twenty minutes over time. But if all we ever got was that day and a half of sensory regulation? I'd be happy."

Royal grinned. He watched Sophie and her student in the ring and his heart swelled. "She's pretty special."

"She is." The woman cocked her head to the side and studied him. "You're her husband?"

"Boyfriend." He considered the word "husband." He would be okay with that. It was probably a ways down the road—they hadn't been together very long. "But hopefully we'll get to husband before too much time passes."

"Are you a Hewitt?"

"Yes. You know my grandparents?"

"I do. They're special, too." She waved to her son as he trotted past.

"They really are."

Sophie reached for the lead as the horse trotted past and, together with the boy, they slowed the horse. "Good job, Matt. Eight minutes this week. New high score."

"Yeah!" He held his hand out and Sophie slapped it. The boy turned. "Did you hear, Mom? Eight minutes!"

"I did! I'm so proud of you." The woman practically glowed, she was beaming at her son so fiercely.

Royal's heart gave a tug. His mom had always been there for him in just the same way. She cheered him on, no matter what struggles he was facing. She hadn't deserved so much of what life had brought her—was there any way he could help her now?

"Good job, Matt." Sophie helped the boy dismount and smiled as he raced to the fence and climbed over it before leaping at his mom. She caught him, staggering back a step until Royal caught her.

"Whoa, there. You're going to break your mom, dude. You don't want to do that. Moms are special."

Matt nodded. "Mine's the best."

"You're the best boy, so it's easy." Matt's mom kissed the top of his head. "Ready?"

"Yep!"

"What do you say?"

"Thank you, Miss Sophie! See you next week!" Matt waved manically before his mom herded him to the path and back out toward the main parking area.

"Heya, stranger." Sophie brought Blaze toward the gate.

Royal unlatched it and swung it open. "You've got a big fan in Matt's mom. Trotting, apparently, bought her a day and a half of no meltdowns."

"Really? That's great news. It can be good for sensory regulation." Sophie shrugged. "It doesn't work for everyone, but I'm glad it helped. He's a good kid. Just—"

"Excited?" Royal chuckled. "It was like he spoke in exclamation points."

Sophie laughed. "Pretty much. What brings you out? I know you're busy with Karen's book."

Royal grinned. "You know that dual voice audition we did?"

"Sure." She looked at him, her eyebrows dragging together. "We got it?"

He nodded. "We did! And they didn't even blink at the per

finished hour price I quoted, which is good. I might need to subcontract out the final editing. I want to make sure we provide the highest quality possible."

"Wow." She ran a hand down Cinnamon's neck and absent-mindedly fished in her pocket for an apple slice. "Matt took off without giving him his treat."

"He was excited."

Sophie laughed. "Always. And I guess the horses don't care as long as they still get the apple from someone."

"Speaking of treats." Royal stepped in and slid his arms around her, tugging her close. He lowered his lips to hers and sank into the sensation of loving her.

"Mmm." Sophie stepped back, pressing her lips together. Her cheeks were pink. "Hi."

Royal traced a finger down her cheek. "Hi. After we get Cinnamon settled, can we look at your calendar and schedule some recording sessions?"

Sophie laughed. "Recording sessions. It's surreal."

"Is that good or bad?"

"Good. It's good." She tilted her head to the side and studied him. "You're not going to get sick of spending time with me?"

"Not possible." He wanted to spend every minute of every day with her. Every minute of every night, too. He squashed that thought. This was the first time since he'd come to Jesus that the changes of living for Him were a challenge. A serious one. He wanted marriage. He also knew it was too soon for that—too soon for even talking about that. Sophie hadn't even told him she loved him yet. He was trying—hard—not to let that eat at him.

She chuckled. "We'll see how you feel after a week or two."

"Maybe you're the one who'll get sick of the togetherness."

"Nah. You're easy to be around, Royal." She set Cinnamon's

saddle aside and leaned up to brush her lips across his. "Hand me that brush?"

It was rare that she was the one to initiate a kiss. Oh, sure, she'd always responded—but Royal couldn't stop his grin as he handed her the brush. Maybe she wasn't as far behind in how she felt as he'd originally thought. Not that it would speed anything up, but it sure would be nice to know they were on the same page.

When the horse and his tack were put away, Royal held out his hand.

Sophie laced her fingers through his. "I've got my calendar on my phone."

"Mine is too. But let's go back to my cabin anyway. The couch there is more comfortable than a hay bale." Barely. The "free to a good home" furniture he'd settled on had its ups and downs. But it was temporary. And for all of that, he wasn't fussy.

"Have any snacks? I'm starving." Sophie pressed a hand to her belly.

"I've got PB and J fixings."

"Perfect." Sophie grinned.

Royal stopped and rested his forehead on hers. "I love you, Sophie."

She closed her eyes and tipped her face so her lips met his.

It wasn't the response he wanted. He ached to hear her say the words. But it would do for now.

He prayed he wouldn't have to settle for too much longer.

"So. I hear you've convinced Sophie to do audiobook narration." Mr. Ellison leaned back in his chair at the kitchen table. He'd pushed his plate toward the middle and had tented his hands in front of him. "How's that going?"

Under the table, Sophie reached over and rested her hand on Royal's leg. Royal covered it with his own. He wasn't bothered by her dad's question. Of the commentary that had gone on during lunch after church today, this was some of the more innocuous. "We'll start tomorrow. But her audition was great. I think it was her work that landed us the job."

"I'm sure it was you." Sophie frowned. "I just read what you highlighted."

"No, you didn't. You put feeling into it. It was good. Why do you always sell yourself short?"

Sophie hunched her shoulders.

Mr. Ellison's gaze sharpened. "She does, doesn't she?"

"Yes, sir. I'm hoping I can help her see she doesn't need to." There. It was out. He glanced at Mrs. Ellison out of the corner of his eye and saw her stiffen. "Your daughter is an amazing woman. Talented, bright, and able to succeed at whatever she puts her mind to."

"Somebody's smitten."

Maybe Karla meant to mutter it, but she hadn't kept her voice low enough. Royal turned to smile at Sophie's sister. "You're right. I am. I love Sophie, and I don't really care who knows it."

"And Sophie? Are you in love, too?" Mrs. Ellison's voice was stiff and polite.

Royal frowned. Did she disapprove? Why would she? Unless she'd gone online to look through his old work. Had she spent any time on his more recent uploads? He looked over at Sophie. It was possible she could look more uncomfortable, possibly, but maybe he should save her from having to make a declaration she didn't mean. "She's still thinking about it. It's okay. She can take all the time she needs. That doesn't change how I feel about her."

"I like you, son." Mr. Ellison grinned and nodded once.

"Leave the boy alone, hon. It's a good day when a father can see that both of his girls are loved by men who deserve them. A good day, indeed. It'd only be better if there was chocolate cake for dessert."

Mrs. Ellison's lips thinned. "I made that for the cake walk on Thursday. The fall festival. I told you that."

"Thursday's so far off, that cake'll be dry and sad. Wouldn't it be better to let us enjoy it now, and you could make another on Wednesday? Or even Thursday morning? Think how much better that'll look for the Missions committee." Mr. Ellison sent his wife a pleading look.

"Oh, all right. Honestly, you're like a child." But Mrs. Ellison smiled as she said it and stood. "Would everyone like a slice?"

A chorus of yesses went around the table and Mrs. Ellison preened. Was complimenting her baked goods going to be the way to Sophie's mom's heart? If so, Royal was up for that.

When thick slices of dark chocolate cake had been distributed, Royal took a bite and grinned. "This is amazing, Mrs. Ellison. You're making another one for Thursday?"

"I am now." She glanced at her husband and shook her head. "Because I guess I have nothing better to do."

"I can come help you, Mom, if you want." Sophie hadn't eaten any of her cake yet. Was something wrong?

"If you can, that would be nice. We haven't baked together in a long time." Sophie's mom smiled. "Let me know when works for you."

"I will. I've always liked making this cake."

"You can make this?" Royal squeezed her hand. "I have a kitchen, you know. You're welcome to use it anytime you like."

Everyone at the table laughed.

"I'll keep that in mind." Sophie took a bite of the cake and sighed happily.

"As I recall, you mostly like licking the bowl." Mrs. Ellison shook her head. "You never did heed my warnings about raw eggs."

"Never got sick, either."

"Yes, well, there's a first time for everything." Mrs. Ellison glanced at Karla. "You got sick that time we made cookies."

"I still think that was because I ate so many of them. Raw and cooked. You're just not supposed to eat the equivalent of a dozen cookies in an hour."

Jamie laughed. "I don't know about that. Seems reasonable to me."

"Agreed." Royal raised his hand. "That sounds like the perfect serving size."

"Those were the days." Mr. Ellison patted his still-trim middle. "It'll catch up with you before you know it, boys. Enjoy it while you can."

Mrs. Ellison swatted her husband's arm.

The rest of the time with Sophie's family was easy. Something had broken the stiff barrier of formality—was it the cake? —and Royal had slipped in as an accepted part of the family.

He'd like to keep it that way.

The drive back to the ranch was quiet.

"You okay?" Royal watched Sophie navigate the switchbacks up the mesa where Hope Ranch perched.

"Yeah. I'm good. I wish you hadn't told my family you love me."

"Why?"

She shrugged. "I don't know. It just feels . . . I can't say it back. I don't know how to know."

"It's okay, Soph. Seriously."

"Maybe to you. I want to tell you I love you, Royal. I just need to know it's true first."

He nodded. "I understand that. I promise you, I do. It's okay."

"You're sure?"

He drew an X over his heart with a finger. "Cross my heart."

"I'm sorry."

"Stop it." He leaned over and kissed her cheek. "We're okay."

She smiled at him as she turned under Hope Ranch's arch.

"You have to help me win your mom's cake on Thursday though. Seriously, it's the best thing I've ever eaten."

"You should have said those exact words to her—she'd love you forever."

"I'll hold it in reserve. I think I got some points today for loving you." He winked.

Sophie laughed. "Probably. I think Mom, at least, had given up on anyone ever wanting to. Speaking of moms, how's yours?"

All the joviality drained from Royal and he sighed. "She's mad at me."

"Because of Jade?"

"Yeah. You'd think I'm single-handedly responsible for her existing." He shrugged and tried not to dwell on the hurt that came with thinking of it. "But she did agree to include her in the disposition. Finally."

"That's good, right?"

"It's the right thing to do. I don't know if any of us think it's good. I'm leaving it in God's hands at this point. I don't know what else to do."

"That's it. And those are good hands."

"Yeah." He tried to smile. He'd promised to give his portion of the estate to his mom to get her to agree. He didn't need the money. Sure, it would've come in handy—there were always things to buy—but he also wanted his mom taken care of. "I'm trying really hard not to be angry with Dad for leaving Mom dangling in the wind with no support like this."

"He didn't know he was going to die."

"No one does. But after this spring—why didn't he take care of things after that close call?" Royal shook his head. "Doesn't matter. Mom's going to be okay. Ish. And Jade won't need to sue anyone."

"And the house in Arizona?"

Royal frowned. "She's going to have to sell. We're working on getting her to come out here."

Sophie's eyebrows lifted. "You think she will?"

"I'm not sure how much choice she has." It hurt his heart to push the issue with her. But Indigo's animals were all here now, so it wasn't like Mom could just move down and live with her. And the house wasn't paid for—in fact, Dad hadn't been making the payments like he'd said he was going to. Mom was going to end up in foreclosure if she didn't sell. The smart thing to do was to come to Hope Ranch.

Mom didn't like it. But she was smart enough to know her options were limited.

At least he hoped she was.

22

H alloween dawned with heavy, gray clouds and a forecast calling for three to six inches of snow by noon. Sophie dug through her bin of winter clothes, looking for her scarf. Where had she put it? Aha. She grabbed the thick, purple wool and tugged.

Tomorrow was supposed to get back into the low forties, so the snow wouldn't stick around, but winter was on the way. She needed to carve out time to talk to Betsy—and probably Wayne —about the indoor ring. If they were serious about it, they needed to make those plans now. Was it even possible to get something built this year when they were starting so late? It didn't have to be fancy. It just needed to keep the weather away.

The fall festival had come together faster than Sophie had anticipated. Skye was a master at convincing people to partici-pate. Every ministry from their church, plus a couple of local organizations, had agreed to provide a game of some sort. The buzz on Sunday morning suggested that many were looking forward to attending. And they'd set the start time early enough that those who chose to could still go around and beg for candy in their neighborhoods afterward.

Sophie wasn't going to judge one way or the other. She'd grown up trick or treating and had never seen it as anything more than a chance to put on a costume and get free treats. Some people, she knew, took it into the dark crevices and sought out the evil that was available to be found any day of the year if they were looking for it. So she understood parents who wanted an alternative. But she also understood the childish joy of dressing up and getting chocolate with no hidden agenda. Parenting wasn't for the faint of heart.

Would Royal want their kids to trick or treat?

And whoa. Where had that thought come from?

Except, she could see it. Little miniatures of her and Royal blended together running around in princess dresses and cowboy chaps. Although, if her daughter ended up anything like Sophie, she'd be wearing a lasso, too. Sophie adjusted the mental image to hold only little cow people dancing around with orange buckets overflowing with candy. And there—she added herself and Royal standing back, observing. His arm around her. His lips sneaking over to her ear. Her neck.

She swallowed and shut down the daydream.

He loved her.

Royal would probably be thrilled to hear about her little foray in the imaginary future. But how was she supposed to know?

Before she could stop herself, she grabbed her phone and punched her sister's contact.

"Sophie? You okay?"

Sophie snorted. "I'm fine."

"I just—you never call me. Is Mom okay?"

"She was when I left yesterday with the cake. Geez, Karla. I call you."

"No. You really don't. Not since I started getting serious with Jamie."

Sophie frowned. Was that true? Not like Karla couldn't have called Sophie. Phone signals went both ways. Except that didn't make Sophie any less at fault. "I'm sorry. I'd like to change that."

"I'd like that, too." Karla paused. "Is that why you called?"

Sophie laughed. "No. Actually, I had a question. It's kind of weird, though."

"Hit me. I'll make up an answer even if I don't have one. I know you love it when I do that."

"Ugh. Stop. I said I was sorry."

"You're right. Sorry. What's up?"

"Now I feel stupid."

"Just ask the question already. I do have other things to do today. And my boss frowns on me being on personal calls for long periods of time."

"Right." How could she have forgotten her sister worked a normal job? Was she that out of touch? She took a deep breath. "How did you know you were in love with Jamie?"

"Really?"

"Yes, really. Some of us weren't born with built-in love detectors apparently."

"I don't think any of us were. I'm just surprised. I thought Royal was joking when he said you were still figuring it out."

"Sadly, no. Can you help me?"

"I'd love to tell you there's a big aha moment, but there wasn't. At least, for me. It was a whole bunch of little things— the way I'd miss him when I was doing stupid stuff like grocery shopping. Or the daydreams I'd spin about our future. When I asked Mom—"

"Hold up. You talked to Mom about this?"

"Sure. She and Dad love each other. They've been married a long time. I figured they'd know."

Okay. That made sense. But still. "I never would have thought to ask Mom."

"Yeah, well, you and Mom have a different relationship. Anyway, you remember in youth group how they used to do the eye-rolly thing with 1 Corinthians 13 where you put your boyfriend or girlfriend's name into the verses on love?"

"Gak. Yes." Sophie shuddered. "Wait. Did Mom tell you that too?"

"Yeah. And as cringey as it was when the youth pastor was going on and on about putting the name of your date in there, when it's someone you're serious about it's a lot less awful."

Hmm. Royal is patient. Yeah, yeah he was. Royal is kind. That too. "Okay. I guess I can see that. Is that all?"

"No. I also spent some time praying about the future—not just with Jamie, but in general. And he was always there—sometimes in the forefront, sometimes just a little glimmer on the side. But I realized I didn't want any of my goals to happen if Jamie wasn't there to celebrate them with me."

Sophie nodded.

"You still there?"

Right. Her sister couldn't see her. "Yeah. Sorry. That makes sense."

"So. Are you in love with Royal?"

"You know what? I think I am."

"You should tell him."

"Yeah. I just have to figure out how."

THE SUN WAS SETTING, turning the gloom of a snow day into the different darkness of dusk.

Royal slipped his arms around her from behind and rested his chin on her shoulder. "I'd say this has been a success."

Sophie turned her head and pressed her lips to his cheek.

"Yeah. I think Skye and I are on board for heading it up again next year already. We'll start planning a little sooner."

He chuckled. "The s'mores at the firepit are a hit. Did you get some?"

"Not yet. I was just thinking I should head that way. It'll be my first s'more of the season."

Royal stepped back and took her hand. "Let's go, before they run out."

"The Hewitts never run out of s'mores. It could be their tagline for the ranch."

He laughed. "We should tell them that. 'Hope Ranch: we always have a s'more for you.' It has a ring."

She jabbed him in the ribs with her elbow.

"Oww." Royal grinned. "How was the ring toss?"

"Surprisingly challenging. I figured it was going to be the easy win that everyone sought out, but even the adults had trouble with it." Sophie scooted closer to Royal as they walked. The temperature was dropping a little with the sun. "I think that's why they kept coming back. Did you win Mom's cake?"

"No." Royal grumbled. "Some little kid sneaked the win."

"Sorry."

He shrugged. "It's okay. Your mom said she'd bake me one next week since I was such a good sport about it."

That was about as close to acceptance as Royal was likely to get from her mom. Dad had already said how much he liked Royal. Karla liked him, too. She glanced up at him and everything seemed to click into place. Both Skye and Karla had said to just tell him, straight out, when she knew. She took a deep breath. "I love you, Royal."

He stopped and turned to face her. "You do?"

She nodded.

He pulled her close and brushed his lips against hers. "I'm so glad. I love you, too."

Sophie stretched up and kissed him. She wound her arms around his neck and snuggled close. They might not make it to the firepit for s'mores. And that was okay. She had everything she'd ever hoped for right here with Royal. Maybe instead of using s'mores in the ranch tagline, she should suggest this —"Hope Ranch: come for the horses, stay for the love."

EPILOGUE

Indigo parked the truck and shifted to look at her mom. "You ready for this?"

"No." Elise stared out the window.

Indigo followed where her mom was looking. It had to be her grandparents' house. The buildings behind looked smaller —cabins and a stable. Whereas this low-slung adobe that sprawled across to a meadow had to be the main house. "You've never been here either?"

"No."

Was her mom only going to use single-word replies? Indigo cut the engine and pushed open her door. "Come on. Let's go say hello."

"I can't do this." Elise reached over and gripped Indigo's arm. "How am I supposed to do this?"

Indigo covered her mom's hand. "I'm with you. Everyone but Azure is here, now. We'll help."

"He hated this place. So much." Elise blinked back tears. "I never understood it."

Looking back at the house and the grounds, Indigo tried to picture her father as a small boy, running wild and free here in the mountains. She couldn't quite bring it into focus. Certainly not enough to understand why he'd turned his back and run far away as fast as he could. "Maybe now you will."

"That's not encouraging." Elise pushed her door open and stepped to the ground. "But since we sold the house in Arizona, I don't have a lot of other options."

Indigo was in the same boat. She'd broken the lease on the house she'd been renting with Wingfeather—thankfully the guy who owned it was understanding and hadn't charged a premium. Wingfeather was still out of touch, so she hadn't been able to end things with him in person. Friends in the commune promised they'd give him her letter if he ever showed back up. She wasn't counting on that happening. It didn't matter. She was over him. They'd made no promises. And she and her animals were here now. It was time for a fresh start.

"You made it!" Betsy Hewitt jogged across the driveway, arms open. "Oh, I'm so glad you both came. How was the drive?"

As the miniature hurricane that was her grandmother hugged and herded them toward the house, Indigo looked around, taking in the surroundings. A tall, lanky man loped around the corner of the house, and her gaze zeroed in on him.

Hmm. As long as that wasn't her sister's fiancé, things were definitely starting to look up. Maybe relocating to Hope Ranch wasn't such a bad thing after all.

A NOTE FROM ELIZABETH...

Royal and Sophie are on the right path for a permanent future together, but they're taking their time and not rushing toward the altar. Being at Hope Ranch together will definitely give them space to solidify their love—and Sophie won't have to wait long for that ring.

In the mean time, Indigo has arrived at the ranch to settle in with all her animals and her fiber business. Joaquin has been a big help with the initial move...will the two of them find they have a lot in common once Indigo's at Hope Ranch full time? Read Hope Ranch book 4 - Hope for Freedom - to find out!

ACKNOWLEDGMENTS

Thank you so much for spending time at Hope Ranch! When I first started this series, I only knew that I wanted to find a way to revisit northern New Mexico - the place I spent the first 11 years of my life and which will always be the home of my heart. I hope that I do it justice and that you get a little taste of the Land of Enchantment. Maybe you'll visit some day — Taos, and many of the places I mention are very real. Hope Ranch is not, but there are many mesa-top meadows that would give you a feel for the place should you visit them.

I couldn't write without the ongoing support of my husband and kids. I'm so grateful they give me time to sit with my laptop and visit the worlds in my head. My sister is a constant encouragement and always has the best feedback - even though I write kissing books.

I'm also grateful for the help and encouragement of author friends! Valerie Comer, Lynnette Bonner, Leslie McDaniel, Tara Grace Ericson, and Heather Gray specifically. Y'all are amazing.

Finally, thanks to Jesus for giving me story ideas and helping the words come. It's my prayer that above all else, my stories are a fragrant offering to You.

WANT A FREE BOOK?

If you enjoyed this book and would like to read another of my books for free, you can get a free e-book simply by signing up for my newsletter on my website www.ElizabethMaddrey.com

OTHER BOOKS BY ELIZABETH MADDREY

Hope Ranch Series

Hope for Christmas

Hope for Tomorrow

Hope for Love

Hope for Freedom

Peacock Hill Romance Series

A Heart Restored

A Heart Reclaimed

A Heart Realigned

A Heart Redirected

A Heart Rearranged

A Heart Reconsidered

Arcadia Valley Romance – Baxter Family Bakery Series

Loaves & Wishes

Muffins & Moonbeams

Cookies & Candlelight

Donuts & Daydreams

The 'Operation Romance' Series

Operation Mistletoe

Operation Valentine

Operation Fireworks

Operation Back-to-School

Prefer to read a box set? Find the whole series here.

The 'Taste of Romance' Series

A Splash of Substance

A Pinch of Promise

A Dash of Daring

A Handful of Hope

A Tidbit of Trust

Prefer to read a box set? Get the series in two parts! Box 1 and Box 2.

The 'Grant Us Grace' Series

Wisdom to Know

Courage to Change

Serenity to Accept

Joint Venture

Pathway to Peace

Prefer to read a box set? Grab the whole series here.

The 'Remnants' Series:

Faith Departed

Hope Deferred

Love Defined

Stand alone novellas

Kinsale Kisses: An Irish Romance

Luna Rosa (part of A Tuscan Legacy)

Non-Fiction

A Walk in the Valley: Christian encouragement for your journey through infertility

For the most recent listing of all my books, please visit my website.

ABOUT THE AUTHOR

Elizabeth Maddrey is a semi-reformed computer geek and homeschooling mother of two who lives in the suburbs of Washington D.C. When she isn't writing, Elizabeth is a voracious consumer of books. She loves to write about Christians who struggle through their lives, dealing with sin and receiving God's grace on their way to their own romantic happily ever after.

BB bookbub.com/authors/elizabeth-maddrey